Where the Daybreak Ends

Stories from Buzzard's Edge

Praise for the Buzzard's Edge Saga

Noose

"Grabs you by the neck from page one and it's full steam ahead 'til the end of the line."

> \- Brian McAuley, author of *Curse of the Reaper*

"*The Batman* meets *Django Unchained*. LaFaro takes to the west with this story of revenge and blood."

> \- Scott J. Moses, author of *Our Own Unique Affliction*

"If you like a revenge tale done right, hop on the next train to Buzzard's Edge. You won't be disappointed!"

> \- John Durgin, bestselling author of *The Cursed Among Us*

"Burning with loneliness and small-town insularity, *Noose* is a chilling addition to the western horror genre. A vicious ear-worm that will keep you humming long after you put the book down."

> \- Lee Murray, USA Today Bestselling author and 4-time Bram Stoker Award-winner

"*Noose* is a gritty yarn of strange violence and loss, of regret and brutal revenge, with dark blood running through its twisted heart. I love a weird western and this is a damn good one."

> \- Alan Baxter, award-winning author of *Sallow Bend* and *The Gulp*

The Demon of Devil's Cavern

"Elements of horror and fantasy pop up in this genre-blurring story about family, loyalty, and good versus evil."

> \- *Booklist*

"*The Demon of Devil's Cavern* is a wild ride along some very dark trails in a weird version of the Old West. Fast-paced and highly entertaining. Brennan LaFaro comes out with both guns blazing!"

> \- Jonathan Maberry, NY Times bestselling author of *Cave 13* and *The Sleepers War*

"With *The Demon of Devil's Cavern*, LaFaro snaps the reins taut and keeps the gallop strong. The characters and events herein are scrawled in dust and sap, framed in rawhide and wire and hung on your heart. A full-bore fire-fueled adventure. I had a blast!"

- John Boden, feller what wrote *Snarl*

"*The Demon of Devil's Cavern* moves like a runaway stagecoach, careening toward its inevitable end. LaFaro returns with a worthy successor to *Noose*, upping the ante with more bullets, more bodies, and more supernatural strangeness. Buzzard's Edge might not be a place you'd want to live, but it's sure fun to visit."

- Josh Rountree, author of *The Legend of Charlie Fish*

"There's a new sheriff in town—and also plot twists, supernatural evils, and mad scientists galore. In this riveting sequel to *Noose*, LaFaro weaves multiple genres into the standard Western mythos. The result? One hell of a tale."

- Drew Huff, author of *Free Burn*

"LaFaro returns to the world of Buzzard's Edge with both six shooters reloaded and ready to fire. *The Demon of Devil's Cavern* sees LaFaro at his best, combining the western horror adventure of *Noose* with all the heart of his *Slattery Falls* trilogy for his best book yet."

- John Lynch, author of *The Warrior Retreat*

WHERE THE DAYBREAK ENDS

STORIES FROM BUZZARD'S EDGE

BY BRENNAN LAFARO

Books by Brennan LaFaro

Buzzard's Edge Saga

Noose
The Demon of Devil's Cavern
Where the Daybreak Ends

Slattery Falls

Slattery Falls
Decimated Dreams
The World You Loved
I Will Always Find You

Standalone

Last Stay
Illusions of Isolation: Thirteen Stories

Where the Daybreak Ends
Copyright 2024 © Brennan LaFaro

All opinions expressed by characters in relation to magic and religion are their personal opinions and are subject to the rules of their universe, which are different from the rules of ours. No characters are scholars in this area, and all are simply coming from a place of trying to do good.

Formatted by: Stephanie Ellis
Cover illustration by: Val Halvorson

First Edition: December 2024

ISBN (paperback): 978-1-963355-20-8
ISBN (ebook): 978-1-963355-19-2

BRIGIDS GATE PRESS
Overland Park, Kansas
www.brigidsgatepress.com
Printed in the United States of America

Content Warnings

All stories contain elements of profanity, violence, murder, and gore. Please see below for story-specific content.

The Reaping - child murder, murder of spouse, animal attack

They Only Come Out at Night - ableism

Come and Take My Hand - child abuse, domestic abuse, implied sexual abuse

Holes - sexual assault, sex (consensual), extreme violence

Where the Daybreak Ends - homophobia, religious zealotry

Trade Secrets - death by flaying

Salvia Sunset - no additional warnings

The Ice Man - suicide

When It's All Said and Done - sex work

For every reader who's braved the harsh heat and dastardly dangers of Buzzard's Edge so far. Let's dig a little deeper, shall we?

Contents

Author's Note	1
Pick a Card	3
The Reaping, Part I	9
They Only Come Out at Night	15
The Reaping, Part II	25
Come and Take My Hand	27
The Reaping, Part III	47
Holes	49
The Reaping, Part IV	61
Where the Daybreak Ends	63
The Reaping, Part V	77
Trade Secrets	79
The Reaping, Part VI	93
Salvia Sunset	95
The Reaping, Part VII	111
The Ice Man	115
The Reaping, Part VIII	147
When It's All Said and Done	151
The Reaping, Part IX	169
Afterword	171
About the Author	175
Lagniappe	177
Spokes in a Wheel	179
More from Brigids Gate Press	181

AUTHOR'S NOTE

Whenever I read a collection, I always assume the author/editor sweated over the order of the stories. In a way, I did that here. The pieces in this book appear in chronological order, not in the order they were written, but the order they happen in the town of Buzzard's Edge. There is a wraparound element present that works best when read in sequential order. Far be it from me to tell you, the reader, what to do, but *Where the Daybreak Ends* was intended to be read from the first page to the very last.

As always, this is a work of fiction where monsters lurk in the shadows, the dead don't always stay that way, and witches conjure magical things, so I've taken some liberties with geography and history.

PICK A CARD

An Introduction to *Where the Daybreak Ends*

Years ago, in another lifetime, I played guitar in a rock 'n' roll band. We had the opportunity to go on tour for several months with another band, and one night in the Green Room of some club, the bass player for the headlining band—let's call him, Paul—started doing magic tricks. All the band members gathered around to watch Paul snatch a coin from behind someone's ear, or make a specific card materialize in the deck upside down. And he did this every night. Incredible sleight of hand tricks I could never figure out, no matter how closely I watched.

One night, I told Paul how much I admired his skill, and he said, "Those aren't even my best tricks." So, I asked if he'd show us his "best" one. Paul replied with a sly smile, "Not until the last night of the tour."

"Why then?"

"Because," Paul said, "after you guys see that one, you won't want to be around me anymore."

He continued giving us an impromptu magic show every night, but we couldn't wait to witness the trick so mind-bending we wouldn't see Paul the same way.

A few weeks later, on the final night of the tour, all the band members and crew gathered around a small table backstage as Paul took out his deck of cards and shuffled them. With a typical magician's flair, he talked about how he could only do this big trick once because it took a lot of psychic energy. He said he'd get a horrible migraine every time he did it.

It started as a simple trick: he fanned out the cards, asked me to pick one and not show it to him. Between my thumb and forefinger, I pinched the nine of clubs, showed it to the other guys crowded around, and slid the card back into the deck. Paul shuffled again, then held the deck up in one hand, keeping his other hand a good eighteen inches away. The fingers started wiggling on that free hand, opening and closing as if they were beckoning. Paul's eyes clenched tight, like he was in pain. We all watched, unblinking, as a single card shivered inside the deck. A corner slipped out, then a quarter, then a half. By then we could all see it was the nine of the clubs.

I was disappointed at first. A great trick, no doubt, but not the tapping-into-the-vibrations-of-the-universe illusion I expected.

That is, until the whole card slid free of the deck and floated in the air halfway between both of Paul's hands. His fingers kept moving, holding the card in place as it hovered, his face and eyes contorted as if it were taking everything he had to make this lightweight playing card defy gravity.

With his eyes still closed, Paul whispered, "Wave your hand around the card in a circle. There aren't any strings."

As I stared at this bass player/magician, I did what he asked and sliced my hand through every inch of air surrounding the floating card. Nothing. No strings, nothing to support the card. That's when some of the people behind me gasped. Paul performed the trick, but then allowed us to believe it wasn't a trick at all.

He slowly, invisibly guided the card back into the deck, and we all erupted into cheers and applause. Without a word, Paul stood and walked through the crowd, head grasped in his hands as if he was trying to keep his skull from splitting apart.

And what do you know? Paul was right. Some of the guys who witnessed the trick were genuinely freaked out. They couldn't find an explanation for how Paul did what he did, and that intellectual blank space was right next door to fear.

As for me, I loved the trick. I loved the fact I was sitting less than two feet away from Paul and I still had no idea how he'd pulled it off.

Every story is a magic trick. An illusion. The writer conjures a world, populates it with characters and ideas, locations and events, and invites a reader to participate in the illusion. Because that's the true magic of a story—it requires participation. What the writer envisions, and what the reader actually experiences will be very different. Oh, what the characters say and do will remain, but what those characters look like, the places they travel, and even their deepest motivations will be supplied by the reader.

A story is a unique magic trick because the "volunteer" called up on stage is not a tool for the magician, but a vital component of the illusion.

in fact, it cannot work without this volunteer. And Brennan LaFaro pulls not just one, but multiple tricks within this wonderful collection.

There are different ways to build the world of a book. Some writers construct as they tell the story, revealing pieces of a larger framework. This works especially well when the story involves another time (past or future) or a societal structure that's unfamiliar.

Other writers give you the sense that the world is already built, already created, and they invite you to let the other world, the "real" world, melt away while you're in this story. A wardrobe to a snow-covered forest with witches and fauns.

With his Buzzard's Edge stories, Brennan LaFaro has created a vivid and colorful version of the Old West that feels both familiar and fantastic. You'll recognize elements from other western stories and movies, but they've been put into a centrifuge and blasted with particles from modern horror, comic books, and mythology into something new and inventive.

Maybe we should stop here for a second so I can ask you a question. You've read *Noose*, right? And *The Demon of Devil's Cavern*? Okay, if you haven't read those two books yet, put this down and order them right now, read them, and come back to this introduction. Don't worry, I'll wait. If you have read those books, then let's proceed, shall we?

Where the Daybreak Ends is precisely the kind of book that will frustrate the uninitiated, but it isn't really for them anyway. It's a gift to all the fans who connected with Rory Daggett and his adopted daughter, Alice. Actually, now that I think about it, maybe you can read *Where the Daybreak Ends* first. I mean, a good story is a good story, and this collection is filled with them. But, even if these stories stand on their own, I highly recommend reading the other books first, and here's why:

In *Noose*, LaFaro created a fictional Arizona town called Buzzard's Edge. It's packed to the saloon doors with ne'er-do-wells, thieves, killers, restless spirits, and dark magic. Maybe even the dirt of the town itself is corrupted in some way. We meet a young Rory Daggett and follow him on a mission to avenge the death of his parents. Little does he know, the titular villain pals around with a gang of criminals torn right from the pages of a 1950s *Batman* comic, only way more bloodthirsty.

We come to know this town, harsh and dangerous though it may be. It feels like a place you've seen, or visited, or maybe just imagined in the kind of dreams that feel like unmade film scripts, shined directly onto the movie screen of your mind.

Buzzard's Edge is not the kind of town populated with tropes and cardboard cutouts. In fact, quite the opposite. Every time we meet a new character—whether it's a bartender, a brothel owner, a sheriff, a teacher, a miner, a seamstress, or a bank teller—we get the sense that this is a fully formed character with history and motivations. Each one suggests complexity and individuality.

For example, in *The Demon of Devil's Cavern*, there are two characters mentioned only in passing. We know their names and where they lived but nothing more. But here, in *Where the Daybreak Ends*, LaFaro gives us their backstory, and surprise, surprise, even the people haunting the edges of this town are fully-realized.

In the story "They Only Come Out at Night," a carpenter and a schoolteacher encounter otherworldly creatures, and in "Salvia Sunset" a group of miners set loose something monstrous from the ground. Throughout literature, there have been a number of towns made famous by how they seem to be intersections between the real world and that of the supernatural. LaFaro is doing his absolute best to make sure Buzzard's Edge earns its place in the pantheon of such haunted locales. Places in which the people are often as deadly and venomous as the creatures that stalk the night.

In *The Demon of Devil's Cavern*, we met a colorful character named Thaddeus Locke, and after witnessing him commit an act of violence with cold efficiency, Rory Daggett ponders what kind of secret life the man may be hiding. Well, in the story "Trade Secrets" we get to see Mr. Locke as he arrives in Buzzard's Edge, and we learn that there is, indeed, much more to him than anticipated.

In many ways, this incredible collection is reminiscent of Rod Serling's *Night Gallery* series. The way he'd walk past a framed painting and tell us the story behind it. All the suspenseful and gory details the painting only hinted at. LaFaro pulls the same kind of magic trick here: taking a multitude of well-drawn characters (and some new ones as well) from the other books, pulling them to center stage, and turning the spotlight on them. He then proceeds to tell us a story about the individual and their connection to this strange, violent, and haunted town.

And the same way you can enter a town from multiple roads, you can come into this series from any direction. It's not strictly necessary to read them in order, although I highly recommend it, as this collection contains secrets, reveals, and revelations regarding characters you come across in the novellas. And for those of you who are already LaFaro devotees, you'll find some fun connections to his other work.

Although these stories are part of the western genre through and through, and proudly so, they also … I hesitate to use the word "transcend" because that implies westerns are somehow *less than*, but the genre is a sandbox and LaFaro is not only playing in it, but assembling those dusty grains into complex structures that flirt with so many genres and sub-genres while remaining true to all the core elements you expect from stories that take place in the Old West, that these stories, in some ways, defy categorization.

Within these pages there are touches of Bradbury, nods to King, and tips of the hat to Lansdale. There is fear, darkness, violence, broken people, wounded souls, hope, humor, and even some romance … just like a real town. A reader can only care about a story's characters if the writer cared about them first. And maybe that's LaFaro's greatest magic trick of all.

Okay, if the stories of *Where the Daybreak Ends* are the destination, then this introduction is just a roadmap. I've marked a few of the dangers but not all of them, because the trip is the adventure, isn't it? So hop on board, hand the conductor your ticket, and settle back as the train starts to rumble down the tracks. Look out the window as the landscape blurs into someplace unfamiliar. A nowhere town baking under the desert sun, haunted by both the living and the dead.

Tyler Jones
Portland, Oregon
April 12th, 2024

THE REAPING, PART I

Josiah Dennis steps out of the shade and into the desert sun. A hatchet, still streaked with days-old blood, hangs listlessly by his side; his only defense against inhospitable conditions and phantom beasts. At least one sunset has passed since he last tasted water, but the dizziness and occasional blackouts make it hard to be sure of the true number. One of these times he may collapse in the brightness of the day and that will be the end.

It's been even longer since he's had food. There's not much out here to strike down with the hatchet, and even the small, skinny creatures run fast.

The crunching sand underfoot is a maddening metronome that begins to slow with the passing time and the heat of the day, as if transitioning to a new movement of a song.

"Come on and sit a spell."

Deep and steady, the voice comes from nowhere and everywhere all at once. One last crunch as Josiah skids to a stop in the middle of the fucking desert. A hundred or so paces behind him, a small sprout of trees sway in a nonexistent wind. They are barely large enough to hide a jackrabbit. Sand as flat as a blacksmith's bench stretches in every other direction. Bright blue sky hangs overhead with a white-hot sun looking over his shoulder.

"Nothing." The word scrapes up Josiah's throat, scratching over his bone-dry tongue, nearly getting caught on the way. It's so raw he only thinks the next part.

There's nothing out here except death.

The hatchet tugs at his hand and, for the first time, he considers dropping it. Leaving it behind. It even starts to slip through his fingers, rasping against his dry snake-like skin until he catches it and holds it tight.

My only protection, my burden.

Something glints in the distance and, at first, Josiah suspects he's imagined it. Easier to believe that nothing helpful could exist in this hellscape.

Then it happens again, no more than a hint of hope. Still, it's more than he's seen in days, so he sets out in that direction.

A shadow, sharp as a dagger, slices by his feet. He need not look up to confirm his fears. A vulture. Not many out here in this arid and unforgiving land. The bird's shadow drifts in a lazy circle, waiting for him to drop dead so it can swoop down and feast unbothered.

Josiah squeezes the handle of the hatchet, feels dried flakes of blood crumble against his fingers.

The shine in the distance catches his attention once more, as if afraid he may have forgotten. Closer now, the way it shimmers reminds him of water. Would that he could be so lucky.

The open desert stretches on in a manner most unlike the land to the east. Back home, rocks and trees give way to mountains and hills; a landscape seemingly designed to entertain as well as enrich. In the desert, everything is monotony and doom. No matter how quickly you move, the land stills around you. As if alive, biding its time. The glimmer remains an impossible dream.

The vulture passes overhead once more.

Josiah listens for the return of the voice, but it is notably absent. Perhaps its owner is watching this half-dead husk of a man amble across scorched sand in hopes that the horizon holds salvation. Perhaps this makes the owner laugh.

The voice of God?

He shakes his head.

No, he thinks. *Just heat, dehydration, and the weight of the world. That, and a touch of imagination.*

The beacon shines at regular intervals and, off in the distance, something else appears. Only a small lump at first, then it grows to the size of a stone, a shrub, a man as he nears. Its features come into sharp relief. Two pointed ears atop a furry body sitting at attention.

Josiah's heart skips a beat.

A coyote.

Contrary thoughts battle in the back of his mind. The possibility of food combats the idea of danger. Fight or flight.

"Onward, Josiah."

The same voice as before, with not a soul to be found. A mangy buzzard overhead and a coyote before him that may be as hungry as he.

And yet the voice soothes. There is no cunning to be found in the words, rather they slide over him like a balm, encouraging his forward progress.

At the edge of the horizon, the coyote waits. The enticing shimmer flickers off its gray fur and leads Josiah's gaze toward the pool at its side.

Only water can make the light dance like that.

Josiah licks his cracked lips. He wants to run, but his legs won't obey. Perhaps exhaustion, perhaps caution. The coyote watches him approach.

The land moves, shrinks, carrying Josiah closer to salvation and bringing the pool into focus. Crystal clear elixir of life, tempting him forward. Surely, the coyote guarding its edge will not mind sharing.

With the watering hole a stone's throw away, Josiah's legs collapse. He crawls through the sand. The coyote watches with curiosity glowing in its eyes.

Let it, Josiah thinks. *If I turn and run now, I'm as good as dead, anyway.*

Josiah drags his body through the sand, inches at a time. When he reaches the water's edge, he plunges his hands in, expecting a trick. Instead, his fingers find icy cold nectar that defies the heat of the day. He slurps the water from his shaking hands. Tears form as the drink cools his throat.

"There. That must hit the spot." A different voice this time, higher and with something like a twang. Each syllable sounds like a plucked fiddle string.

Josiah lifts his head and finds the coyote still resting on its haunches, staring at him.

"Did … did you say something?"

The coyote tilts its head and opens its mouth. "The water," it says. "Gotta be refreshing after your journey."

The world spins and Josiah's mind races. *I've died,* he thinks. *I've died and this is my eternal reward. Or torture.*

A soft clump shakes the ground as the vulture he's seen circling overhead plops onto the sand a few feet away. It stretches its wings, then tucks them close. "You don't look so good, friend." That deep voice, with just the hint of a tremble.

Josiah swears he can see concern in its strange eyes. One midnight black, the other a milky haze.

"You can't talk." He stammers the words as he watches the coyote and the vulture trade a knowing look. "You can't talk," he repeats. "What the hell kind of place is this?"

The coyote speaks first. "Buzzard's Edge. Though you should know, the name wasn't exactly unanimous."

The vulture lets out a caw that could almost pass for laughter.

Looking around, Josiah sees nothing. Just open land, beaten by the unforgiving sun of the western territories.

"There's nothing here," he whispers.

"I don't know 'bout that," says the coyote. "If you let yourself stare off into the distance, eventually it'll form. Not unlike the watering hole, I reckon."

Josiah squints, willing something to form on the horizon. Nothing does. Only swells of sand, reaching for eternity.

"I don't—"

Waves of haze shimmer off the sand, damming Josiah's words. They dance across open air until a shape appears. Gradually, as if Josiah has crawled closer to it. A grin spreads across his face. More shapes emerge behind the first. Dark and clean-cut. Lines too straight to belong to natural fixtures. Buildings. A town.

"There it is," says the coyote, with a mix of awe and humor. "And guess who was here to watch S first sprung from the ground?"

"Not to mention who'll be here when it crumbles to dust, lost to time," adds the vulture.

The animals smile, as much as animals can smile.

"How could you know that? What is to come?" Deep in the recesses of his mind, Josiah feels absurd, conversing with bird and beast, yet the clarity of the moment stifles his embarrassment.

Let them explain themselves, he thinks.

Silence lingers for a moment and, at first, Josiah thinks they will not answer. Perhaps they were never able to answer.

Then the vulture speaks.

"This is an unusual land," it says. "Demanding. And there are good sides and bad sides to that. It spills its secrets to those who pay attention to past, present, and what is to come."

"Past, present, and what is to come," echoes Coyote.

"Time is stacked up and in line most often," continues Vulture, "but sometimes it overlaps. It falls to Coyote and myself to keep the stories."

Something about the authority in the vulture's voice frightens Josiah. His pulse races and his stomach aches. For the first time since the coyote spoke, he remembers the hatchet at his side.

"Are the stories meant for you alone?"

Once again, the animals passed an unreadable look.

"What good is a story that cannot be shared?" The vulture stares at Josiah, its cloudy eye swirling like mist. "What is your name?"

Josiah tells them.

"Come on and sit a spell, Josiah," says Vulture.

"Be happy to share one," says Coyote.

Josiah helps himself to some more water, then nestles between the two animals. He lays the hatchet down, within reach, but out of his hands. Suddenly, everything feels lighter. Josiah Dennis stares across the bleached sand, watching the town grow, as Coyote begins to speak.

THEY ONLY COME OUT AT NIGHT

"Howdy … s-strangers," called Ned Callaghan, shaking the second word loose as he descended the rough-hewn schoolhouse steps. He squinted against the dusk as it teased three wraith-like silhouettes, wrapped in long coats. Moon-white faces peered from beneath wide-brimmed hats. They stood, as if waiting, at the Buzzard's Edge line. The words fluttered through the air, drifting past the shadowy forms, before the desert swallowed them.

Ned let his hammer hang by his side as his gaze wandered away from the strangers, crawling over the surrounding buildings before returning to the schoolhouse, the fruit of his labor. Only a few days from finished by his estimate. If the burgeoning civilization of Buzzard's Edge were a baby, it wouldn't be old enough to give up the tit. Wanderers from the hills frequently stumbled into town, had since the first hint of construction, for the promise that someday, an oasis might grow out of the wooden skeletons and sand, to give a group of refugees and undesirables a place to call home.

Something seemed off about these visitors, however. Maybe the silence with which they conducted themselves, or the way they stood so still, in defiance of the evening wind. It made Ned nervous, but then, that wasn't nothing new. Half the reason he'd set out west in the first place.

The stranger in the center stepped forward, glanced toward its feet, and seemed to decide that was far enough.

"Rest," it said, or so Ned thought. The voice hissed, more reptile than man. *Like a snake choking out a cat.* A shiver danced across his shoulders.

"R-rest," repeated Ned, trying out the word. "Well, now, if you f-fellas need to get off your f-feet for the night, M-Maude's m-might be your best bet." He wiped a line of sweat from his brow.

The three stared, tilting their heads in unison in a way that made Ned's blood run cold.

Too perfect. Unnatural.

Silence lingered in the air as the sun ducked behind the horizon. The three figures made no move either in advance or retreat.

"Or … or just s-stay out there and … and f-freeze," mumbled Ned. He lowered his voice in order to keep his snark to himself but couldn't help worrying the trio might've caught his words. He almost laughed until it struck him how empty the streets were. The faint hint of a good time drifted over from Maude's, everyone else in Buzzard's Edge having packed in their work for the day. Nearly dropping his hammer trying to get it through his belt loop, Ned decided to call it quits as well.

"Good … good luck, gentlemen. W-wish you the b-best of luck." He even tipped his hat as he backed toward the heart of town, afraid to take his eyes off the outsiders.

Another hiss came, but if it was supposed to represent a word, Ned couldn't guess what that word might be. Their forms blended into the gloom beneath the cold moonlight. The farther he got, the less sure he became of being watched.

Only he *was* sure. Their gaze landed on his back the same way you felt it when someone had a gun trained on you.

"N-nothin' … nothin' f-for it," he whispered to himself. Half tempted as he was to warm his blood with a pint from Maude's, the idea of walking through those batwing doors and catching a room full of stares steered him in the direction of home.

Relief set in at the sight of his modest abode, nestled snug in the middle of town just up the hill from the outskirts and far from the prying eyes of the ghost-like drifters. Ned wrapped himself in an extra layer of blankets.

Buzzard's Edge chilled a little harder than usual that night.

Come.

The word echoed through Violet Conway's mind unbidden. So faint she didn't even put her book down. A simple shake of her head, then she tapped the page to find her place and kept going.

Dying firelight flickered across the pages, matched by the final traces of the setting sun. Just enough leftover light to draw a dim outline of the buildings.

So much progress in a relatively short period of time.

With a sigh, she closed her book, imagining the desolate, uninhabited patch of land that had sprawled in the shadow of the mountains only a few short years earlier. She squinted to make out the various buildings in the retreating glow, finally settling on the schoolhouse. It was slightly taller than the surrounding structures, with a bell tower resting on top.

For months, Ned Callaghan had toiled away to give the children of Buzzard's Edge a place to learn. To give Miss Conway a place to teach them. She'd passed by on occasion, flashed him a smile, and received one in return. The work appeared to be going well, nearing completion any day now.

Maybe she would stop by to see him the next day.

Come.

Violet frowned. That word again. Still soft, almost drowned out by her father snoring in the other room, but with a sense of intrusion. Like her mind hadn't been responsible for conjuring the idea.

A chill raced up her arms, leaving hairs standing in its wake. An overwhelming urge to cover the windows grew in her. To keep something from getting in. No, that wasn't right.

To keep it from *seeing* in.

Heart racing, Violet laid her book on her night table, taking care not to let it make a sound, then padded across the room, barefoot and on the tips of her toes. As she covered the gaping windows with canvas tarp, a warmth unrelated to the hearth fire seeped back into her bones. Still striving for silence, she slipped back into the chair.

Come.

The voice tickled at the back of her mind once more, barely more than a whisper this time.

Bright and early, Ned set back to work, building a railing along the stairs that led to the new schoolhouse. Before he drove the first nail in, he scanned the horizon.

Not a soul in sight.

All too quickly, the day passed. As dusk loomed closer, Ned kept half his attention on the town line.

"Sun's gone down, Mr. Callaghan, and look at you, still sweatin' up a storm."

Fixed as he was on the approaching darkness, Ned's heart missed a beat, then pounded double hard to make up for it. His mind often moved faster than his mouth, and it only took a moment to realize that the voice—light and lilting—did not resemble a hiss.

"S-sakes alive, Miss Violet. You just about got my heart s-stuck in my throat."

Violet knit her brows in concern. It only made her look prettier, and Ned had a hell of a time keeping a goofy grin off his face.

"I … I just mean you s-scared me is all."

Violet's face softened, her brow relaxing like hair let down after a long day of being tied up. She opened her mouth to reply, but a harsher voice cut her off.

"Ey, Callaghan, try not to let any of that stammer seep into the woodwork."

Jim Taggert approached from behind Violet, circled around her and leaned against the railing, driving his shoulder into it as if to test the durability. Contrary to the shy smile that had graced Ned's lips before falling flat, Taggert's smug grin beamed bright enough to make a person forget the night was on its way. "New frontier and all, last thing we need's a group of idiotic kiddies what can't speak the right way."

Ned flapped his lips. Only the words didn't come. Maybe for the best. He had no idea what they would have been. He went a hot shade of red, knowing he looked like a salmon caught on a riverbank. His cheeks darkened to crimson when Taggert shook with laughter, belting it out so hard he had to lean over and brace his hands on his knees.

"Jim Taggert," said Violet, with a fire in her voice the same quality as that in Ned's cheeks. "You're one to talk about folks receiving a proper education, you halfwit. Now fuck off on home. Leave those be that put in a hard day's work, rather than tippin' back moonshine and grousing for a soiled dove to go searching through your britches for a hint of a prick."

Ned expected Taggert to get angry, maybe show some shame, but he blanched the same pale white as the strangers on the outskirts, and his mouth went deadly straight.

"You talk to the kiddies that way, Violet?" Taggert shook his head. "Fine woman like you ain't gonna amount to much with a fuckin' mouth like that. My Pa says a woman only smarts off because she's beggin' for a man to set her straight." He stepped forward and a flicker of a smile returned, laced with cruelty this time around. "So how 'bout it? We find someplace quiet, and maybe I set you straight."

Violet's eyes dashed toward Ned and his heart took off like a dappled mare. She took a deep breath, looking like she was trying not to shake and doing a less than stellar job.

"Fuh … fuck off," said Ned. Deep down he knew tripping over his words made him sound tentative and unconvincing, so he channeled every glowing ember of rage into his eyes and let them make up for the ground where his voice failed him.

Taggert's gaze darted back and forth between Ned and Violet, flitting nervously as a miner watching a box of dynamite near an open flame. After a moment, the cruel grin reached up and touched his eyes, lingering for only a second. He swiped a hand through his hair and stepped back.

"Wouldn't waste my time with Nervous Ned if I was you," he said. "His mind don't work right. You know that." His words lost their weight as he reached the end of the sentence. A smart-ass parting shot rather than a biting insult.

Ned and Violet said nothing as he pounded a fist against the railing and walked away.

Before he rounded the corner, Taggert spun and raised his eyebrows, looking at something behind them. "Looks like we got some prospective new citizens to Buzzard's Edge. If you decide to welcome them in, Violet, maybe try and keep a civil tongue. Don't want any newcomers thinkin' we're monsters."

The hair stood up on the back of Ned's neck, already knowing what he'd find. He bit his lip as he shifted his gaze toward the edge of town.

Tall and gaunt, skeleton thin, and draped in a black so dark it devoured the twilight.

This time there were seven.

"Who are they?" Violet's legs trembled beneath her dress as something about the shadows dotting the horizon stole the warmth from the air. She passed a glance with Ned, but his face had gone ashen. A shake of the head was all he could manage. At least he didn't try to speak this time.

They don't move. Like their feet are trapped in the sand.

As much as she despised Taggert, she wished he would come back, if only so it wasn't two against seven.

"Why don't they come any closer?" Violet only whispered the words but had the sense they traveled farther than intended. "They don't look … right. Have … have you s-seen 'em before?"

Violet's voice mimicked that awkward way Ned had of pausing between words, like the gears in his mind had to click into place before he could spit them out. She found herself turning the color of her namesake.

"Th-they only come out … at night."

"Christ, Ned. That's ominous as hell."

Her hands dangled by her side, swaying in the gentle onset of the night breeze. For a moment, she thought about taking Ned's hand. Would it be rough and calloused, like the boots he wore? Damp with sweat after a day's work? Ned's eyes darted around, as if afraid of accidentally catching her gaze.

Is he thinking what mine might feel like, too?

Facing back toward the dark figures, Violet caught a glint of red beaming from beneath one of their hats.

Eyes, she thought. *Red as fucking fire.*

As if on cue, pinpricks the color of fresh blood burst open on the wan faces of every one of the seven.

Come, a voice whispered. Not from ahead. It was the same as the day before, only louder. It rattled around the inside of Violet's skull, scraping at bone, and digging into her mind like a needle stitching a gaping wound.

Violet took a step toward the invisible line in the sand.

"D-d-don't," cried Ned.

Come.

Ned grimaced, clutching his fists so tightly his knuckles whitened.

"P-please."

Violet's boot caught in the sand. She tensed her muscles, though her leg tried to keep moving forward. Like the grains beneath her foot were evacuating from Buzzard's Edge; a rockslide fleeing down the side of a mountain.

Come.

Ned grabbed her hand. His palm was damp—just like she suspected it would be—shaking. Veins crawled across his forehead like writhing worms. Did he feel the same pull?

Gritting her teeth, Violet squeezed his hand and glared at the seven strangers. The crimson lights flickered, one by one. With every dimmed blood-red light, the pull on her legs, on her mind faded, until the memory became flimsy as onion skin.

The Sonoran Desert swallowed the final semblance of sun and, with it, the wraith-like figures.

Even in their silence, Violet sensed them still.

Come.

Only an echo this time.

"We … y-you should get on home," said Ned, staring at their clasped hands.

A faint smile rested on her lips, and warmth bubbled in her stomach. Her body's attempt to banish the dread to the edge of town.

"You're right," she said. "You working tomorrow?"

"Ev-every day … 'til it's d-done."

"Well, then maybe I'll see you."

She dropped his hand, sliding her fingers across his to make it last, then turned and walked toward home. An icy feeling took hold, like cold water dripping down her back. Their stares, the strangers. She shuddered. Still, she refused to search the night any longer.

That night, Violet shivered beneath her blankets. It wasn't particularly cold, though visions of the red-eyed wraiths cut through her like a harsh winter wind.

Ned's nerves jangled something fierce throughout the next day.

They only come out at night, he kept telling himself, but the Arizona sun provided little comfort.

Violet came by when the sun was at its highest, bringing a few sandwiches and an invitation to retreat to the shade. They ate in silence, nervous eyes searching the horizon, even with evening lurking hours away.

"Why don't you just go on home early? You know they're comin'."

Ned chewed slowly, letting his words swirl into the right order before trying to set them free. "I d-do know that." He brushed crumbs off his hands. "A-and I guess they'd c-come whether I was here or … or not. S-sometimes the best way to … to f-fight the devil is to … to keep a g-good eye on him."

A smile spread across Violet's face. She lowered her head as if to hide it. "Know what I think, Ned?"

He returned the grin. "Wh-what's that?"

"I think those words sound a lot smarter than they actually are."

His lips twitched and he shot her a wink, then went back to his lunch.

When they finished, she gathered up the mess and disappeared for a few hours. He knew she'd be back, though, if only to see if he was really foolish enough to stay.

Sure enough, as the sun started to descend, Violet Conway arrived in the shadow of the schoolhouse, iron at her hip. Under other circumstances, it might have struck Ned strange to see an armed schoolteacher, but Buzzard's Edge was new and dangerous. Its residents carried weapons with as much ceremony as they did hats and coats.

His face brightened to see her, then he frowned at her bloodless pallor. Violet's hand shot to her side, gripping the handle of her pistol, knuckles white as her face.

"V-Violet."

Her gaze passed clear over his right shoulder, and he knew what waited behind him. A sensation like skittering bugs crawled up his spine, and slowly, inevitably, he turned.

Ned's stomach dropped so hard and fast, he was afraid it might slap against something inside him and burst.

Dozens of dark figures straddled the line to Buzzard's Edge. Side by side, leaving barely enough room for a man to pass between.

We're surrounded, he thought. *There's too many. What do they want?*

Violet's pallor gave way to a blush in her cheeks and fire in her narrowed eyes.

"Hey!" she shouted, summoning a bravado Ned could never hope to inject into his own voice. She brushed by him; pistol clear of her holster. He grabbed her arm. She slipped away from his grip, closing the distance by a few steps.

"What are y'all doin' lurking at the edge of town like a bunch of bandits in the night? Either come on in or scram!"

Come. Come. Come. Come. Come.

The word echoed so loud it made Ned feel trapped in a canyon with its ghost. It didn't sound like Violet's voice. Worse yet, it seemed lodged in his head, like a burrowed tick.

The discomfort lasted only a moment, then one by one, hollow red gashes beyond count cut through the darkness. Demonic eyes flickering in haste, until the darkening desert filled with crimson fireflies.

A series of hisses filled the air, like a disturbed nest of rattlesnakes. The shrill noises mimicked human speech, mocking more than imitating.

Come.

That was when the first stranger stepped forward, crossing the town line into Buzzard's Edge.

A rush of black wind blew Violet's hair back, as the red-eyed creatures poured into the streets of Buzzard's Edge, following the lead of the first creature brazen enough to cross the town line. The brush of Ned's fingers still tickled her arm as a midnight-dark mist enveloped them. Thick as brushfire smoke, but without any heat, without the acrid scent of burning.

I can't see!

I should have listened.

I should never have invited them in.

A guttural grunt interrupted her racing thoughts, and a pit formed in her stomach at the possibility Ned might be hurt. Screams sliced through the air. Perhaps from the center of town, though they seemed to engulf Violet. A sheer terror inflicted on the heart of Buzzard's Edge by the devils composed of black smoke with eyes hot enough to brand cattle.

"Ned!"

The roiling darkness choked her words. Desperately, she swung her arms, seeking his hand, his face. Any sign. She pictured Ned groping through the darkness, searching for her in kind, then the barest hint of moonbeam pierced the blackness surrounding them.

My imagination?

She shook her head, though the light was too dim for anyone to notice. Piece by piece, the moon's glow banished the plumes of sooty wind.

The dim light unveiled a pair of boots, the same fatigued grayish brown ones that Ned wore. Her heart skipped a beat and traces of a smile spread across her face.

"Ned!"

No response, except distant shrieks. They told of agony. Then the other sounds crept in. Wet tearing, like one might hear from a butcher shop, combined with pained moans and the hissing sound favored by the strangers. Only it no longer sounded angry, but gleeful.

They're killing everyone, she thought, pulse throbbing in her neck, chest constricting. *And I invited them in.*

Darkness still shrouded her but allowed a glint of hope to shine through. Ned's boots gave way to a faded pair of jeans and an off-white button shirt decorated with splotches of red. Violet's smile slipped as the smoke continued to clear.

Shadows flew overhead, swooping faster than a red-tailed hawk.

By the radiant light of the moon, Ned swayed, his dull eyes locked on Violet's.

"Ned …" Not a shout this time. "Your—"

The drifting smoke consummated into a pale shape fixed to Ned's neck, formless and writhing, until two brilliant red pinpricks opened at its center, studying Violet, challenging her. An unyielding abyss of starless night replaced the stranger's salt-white skin.

"V-Violet." Ned's voice barely pushed past a whisper, softer and with less weight than the vanishing mist. His skin paled before her eyes, losing its healthy tan to a shade that matched the moon.

"You monster!" She drew the gun from her holster and fired before she aimed. Years of target practice and a daddy—*he's still at home. Have they gotten him, too?*—who trained his little girl to survive in the new frontier made her aim true, spared Ned Callaghan's life for the space of a second.

The bullet passed squarely between the creature's eyes, swallowed by a liquid blackness, then disappeared into the night. The creature pulled away from Ned's neck and stood to its full height. She'd never seen a man-shaped figure so tall. Even as it grew, blinding white teeth formed a bastardized version of a smile. Two fangs—*canines*, she thought—stretched to the length of rifle rounds and arrived at gleaming points.

Come in, it hissed, holding Violet's gaze for a second, a minute, maybe forever.

"Violet. Run." Ned's voice broke her stupor.

The beast's ink-black lips curled into a look of annoyance, then it drew them into a ghastly smirk, and wrapped its cadaverous hands around Ned's head. Tendons popped and bone snapped as the creature wrenched skull free from spine, then dropped his disembodied head to the sand, before bursting into a trail of black smoke, riding the wind farther into town.

Screams poured in from the distance, as if heralding the creature's arrival.

Ned's body swayed once more, then fell to the ground.

The mist cleared; curtains pulled back to reveal a hellish stage. Streams of blood ran through the streets of Buzzard's Edge. Eviscerated body parts lay strewn about, carelessly trampled by the dark strangers as they careened from one victim to the next, burying fangs in the necks of people she knew and cared about before snapping their spines and leaving their corpses face-down in the street.

"Help!" screamed Taggert. "Violet, hel—"

Halfway through the word, one of the ethereal beings thrust a hand through Taggert's torso, displaying his still-throbbing heart for a couple of beats before yanking him back into a cloud of shadow.

Amid the tearing noises—*the sound of feasting*, she thought—and the cries, Violet spared only a quick glance toward Ned's desecrated husk, then she turned her back on the bloodthirsty creatures, turned her back on the townspeople pleading for help, and heeded Ned's final word.

She ran.

THE REAPING, PART II

"What happened to Violet?" A dry wind bites at Josiah's wide eyes. Only then does he realize he is on his feet, walking.

Nervous sweat trickles from his brow as his heart hammers in his chest. The hatchet. He recalls laying it on the ground, but now it has returned to his hand.

What sorcery is this?

Before him, the outline of Buzzard's Edge grows larger, clearer. His throat constricts as he recognizes the framework of the tallest building, a bell tower stabbing into the sky.

"That there's the schoolhouse," says Coyote. Its eyes flick toward Josiah. "The very one Ned built, the one Violet woulda taught at 'til …"

"Though it does not yet have a name. And this," says Vulture, "is the town line."

The trio halts as though they've hit an invisible wall.

"The same one those monsters lined up at," whispers Josiah. Tension bleeds into his veins and he stares down the streets of Buzzard's Edge, anticipating bloodsucking creatures in every shadow. The air grows thick.

Vulture unleashes another one of those laugh-like caws. "You'll find you need no invitation to enter here."

Sucking in a deep breath, Josiah steps forward. Nothing attacks. A light breeze settles the air, offering a touch of clarity. Sturdy wooden buildings line the streets, new and barely used. Fresh as a daisy if not for the occasional splash of dried brown. His stomach churns at the thought, the knowledge, of what stained the wood.

"Violet?" he asks once more.

"Well, now," says Coyote, lifting its brows and glancing toward Vulture. "That part gets a little hazy. Some things do when they get too far from this place. When they're pointed this way? Well, that's different. Can tell you for sure that she set out east, ran like the Devil was chasin' her—which, in a manner, he was. S'pose she either made it or she didn't. Never did come back, though."

Josiah wanders toward the schoolhouse, runs a finger along the railing Ned had built in the story. "How long?"

"Pardon?" asks Vulture.

"You said Violet never came back. Those things from the story are all gone. If you're gonna pass it off as truth, how long's it been?"

Vulture cocks its head and stares at Josiah for a moment, two. "Long enough for the girl to either grow older or rot in the desert. Long enough for those creatures to eat everything Buzzard's Edge had to offer, and either die themselves or move on. Does that answer your question?"

"I guess it'll have to," Josiah mutters. Coyote speaks with a friendly, jovial tone, but there is a darkness in Vulture's words that makes him clutch the hatchet a little tighter.

The breeze heightens, murmuring through the empty streets.

"Is there anyone here?" asks Josiah.

"Naught but three souls for the time being," answers Vulture. "But the others will be on their way soon."

A shiver runs along Josiah's skin, raising hairs and chilling sweat.

Coyote sits and stares up at the schoolhouse. "Would it comfort you to hear another story?"

With a tremble, Josiah says, "Is it about monsters again?"

Coyote brays laugher. This time, there is no mistaking it for anything else.

"Josiah Dennis," says Vulture, roosting at the top of the schoolhouse steps. "All stories are about monsters."

Come and Take My Hand

"Time for bed, Georgie." Janie Holcomb leaned on the kitchen table and inclined her head toward the boy's bedroom. "Got to be up with the sun tomorrow and you ain't sleep well last night."

George blinked as if the action could hide the dark circles beneath his eyes. "I couldn't sleep, Mama."

"And why ever not?" Janie crossed her arms and fixed her gaze deeper than George's eyes.

He got the feeling she could study the back of his skull if she so desired.

George shifted his foot, scraping it against the rough floorboard.

"Out with it."

"She's watchin', Mama. That woman I told you 'bout."

Janie lowered her head, eyes squinted and nostrils flared. A moment passed.

"It's true!" George stared down at his feet. "It's like the night gets darker. She sucks up the moon and stars, and then she looks in. Never tries the latch or nothin'. Just … watches, and—"

Janie sighed. "Is that all? George Holcomb, you're too old for such fairy tales to be occupyin' the space between your ears."

"But Mama, she—"

"I won't hear another word about it." Her tone softened and the barest hint of a smile shone through, just enough to display a tooth-sized gap. "You'll be alright, Georgie. Had a bad dream is all. Now get your behind to bed 'fore your father gets home and …" She shook her head and her smile dropped away. A shiver rippled through her shoulders.

It ain't even cold in here, thought George.

"You listen to your mama now." Any trace of anger had deserted her voice. "Go on."

The tiny hairs stood on the back of George's neck as he peeked past the kitchen and into his room. A pulse traveled through the shadows, beckoning. He curled his toes, scraping them against the unforgiving floor. Whatever awaited him paled in comparison to his mother's ire and father's belt. Without a word, he turned and scuttled off toward his room, his mother's stare drilling into the space between his shoulder blades as if in search of oil.

Averting his eyes from the window, George changed clothes in a hurry and threw himself into the bed. Candlelight flickered in from the kitchen, lending motion to the already dizzying array of shadows. He pulled the covers up over his head, breathing fast and hard in the enclosed space. The slight orange glow permeated the thin sheet. At least Mama was still awake and watching over him. When the candle's light-orange hue cut off suddenly, his heart took off like a frightened snake.

Footsteps approached.

"No wonder you're scared of the dark, blanket pulled up over your head and all. Come outta there, Georgie. Let me see that face one more time tonight." Mama's comforting weight settled next to him on the bed.

Reluctantly, George lowered the blanket. "You ever get scared, Mama?"

"All the time, but gettin' older means facing your fears instead of hidin' from 'em." She looked down at her lap. "Of course, facing fears can mean all kinds of things, can't it?"

George lowered his voice to a conspiratorial whisper. "What scares you most?"

"Truth?"

"Of course."

"Something happenin' to you. Sometimes being grown up means meeting your fears head on, but sometimes it means doing everything you can, and that ain't always pleasant, to keep the monsters away from those you love. Know what I mean?"

George nodded, though he wasn't sure he understood.

"If you don't now, you will someday. I'll make sure of it." She stood with a sigh and crossed the room. "Sleep tight, sweet thing."

Mama's words floated across the room, soothing the discomfort that hung in the air. As she left his doorway, the candlelight danced for a moment longer before Janie Holcomb extinguished it. With George put to bed, she'd likely grown tired of waiting for her husband to lumber in from the tavern. Sometimes Father didn't crash through the front door until nearly sunup, but he always came home.

Still hidden beneath the safety of the covers, George's heart slowed to a normal pace. His breathing became deep and steady, peaceful. Sleep lurked at the edges of his vision with outstretched fingers, waiting to take him.

Skreeeeeeeeeeeeek.

Something scratched at his windowpane. Beads of sweat gathered on George's forehead, threatening to fall. He clutched the sheet so tight that his fingernails dug through the thin linen and bit into his palms.

George wanted to stay wrapped in its comforting warmth, but he knew who raked at the window. Time and panic would transform her face into something more terrible than reality. In his imagination, her teeth descended into glistening fangs, eyes yellowed, taking on the vertical slit pupil of a goat, and her already pallid skin dimmed to resemble a chalky white found only in death.

A fairy tale, Mama had said. *Just a fairy tale.* George gritted his teeth and tossed the blankets off. They landed on the wood floor with a soft clump. It was the only sound in the house. He scrunched his eyes shut, but the darkness surrounded him still.

Skreeeeeek.

Shorter and a little softer this time. More like a gentle caress than a threatening note. But still, *she* waited. Not a fairy tale.

Raising one eyelid at a time, George turned his attention to the window. There she was. The woman in the window, draped in fabric so black she was almost lost against the night.

Woman.

George shook his head as though he'd spoken the thought aloud. That wasn't right. She couldn't have been much older than his eleven years. Her skin glowed soft and white, but it told of life rather than death. The girl's light-blue eyes gleamed with sadness, maybe longing. Her pursed lips curved into the ghost of a smile, and relief flowed through him. Those lips were not large enough to hide the imaginary pointed teeth that had filled him with dread only moments ago.

She lifted a hand to the window and pressed her fingertips against the glass. No shrieking scratch this time, only a barely audible tap. The five fingers hung before George, begging his understanding. George's feet carried him across the room without permission, drawn by her icy blue eyes. She never stayed this long the other nights. Always disappeared as if lured away by the light of the moon before he could decide what to do.

Always leaving him wondering if it was a dream or not.

Not this time.

With only the thin glass separating them, the girl lowered her hand and stepped back, waiting expectantly. *Open the window*, said something in George's mind. *Just a crack will do.*

He obeyed.

The sweet and spicy aroma of cinnamon drifted into the room. George offered a shy smile. "Gets awfully cold out here at night. Don't you got no place to sleep?" Before she could answer, he continued, "Mama says all them critters what love the hot sand are ascared of the cold, so you ain't got to worry 'bout rattlers or scorpions when the moon takes over the sky. That why you're out here at this time of night?"

The edges of her smile lifted. When she spoke, her voice was flat and lacked the emotion that lived in her eyes. "Something like that. I prefer to walk at night, avoid the sun, the critters, and the … people."

George cocked his head. "If you're looking to avoid people, coming up and tappin' on a window sure is a strange way to go about it."

"Something always catches my attention when I walk by your house, George. By your window. It's hard to describe, but I guess the best way to put it is … a light."

"Mama usually leaves a candle lit until she gives up and goes to bed, tired of waitin' for my—" George raised his eyebrows. "Say, I don't believe I gave out my name."

"I know."

"Well, seems only fair I should know yours then." He smiled, allowing any lingering nerves to drip away.

"Merella," she said.

"Well, Merella, that's a lovely na—"

Crash.

From the other side of the house, the front door had burst open and clattered against the wall. George's heart climbed up his throat and tried to get a grip on the back of his tongue before it plunged down and plopped into his stomach.

"That's my daddy," George whispered. "He'll be crosser'n a snakebit horse he comes in and sees you. Best you move along."

Merella nodded and George reached to close the window, but hesitated. Footsteps stomped across the kitchen floor. "Wouldn't upset me none if you knocked on my window tomorrow night, though." He flashed a sheepish grin.

"Maybe I will," Merella whispered. Then she vanished as if a hole had materialized in the night air and swallowed her.

George eased the window shut and tiptoed back to bed, pulling the covers up a second before the hulking frame of his father filled the doorway. The scant moonlight glinted off the man's belt buckle, but the rest of him remained enveloped by shadow. Squeezing his eyes shut and attempting to mimic the steady breathing that came with sleep, George said a silent prayer that his father would bypass his room that night. The stink of sweat and grain alcohol filled his nose, relegating the smell of cinnamon to a distant memory. It sent his heart racing even as he felt the piercing gaze on him. After what seemed like hours, the statue in the doorway let out a rumbling belch and stumbled away.

Before long, the familiar babble of muffled pleas, thwacks of leather against flesh, slapping of skin on skin, and animalistic rutting came from the other room. George recited another prayer for his mother, figuring if the first one had worked, maybe the second one might stand a chance.

"Rise n' shine, Georgie."

Janie Holcomb shook George awake before the first beam of Arizona sunshine poured in the window. He wrestled his eyes open, knowing the morning light would peer over the horizon any second.

When it did, he caught a glance of dried blood at the corner of her lip. Only a speck, but it drew his eyes like flies to a horse's behind. Janie wiped at her face, banishing the bloody spot to oblivion.

"Mama."

"Ne'er you mind, Georgie. Get your lazy backside out of bed and go help your father." She raised her eyebrows, but George missed whatever she might be trying to communicate with the gesture. "Don't want to keep 'im waitin'," she whispered.

George dressed quick as a startled bird and dashed outside. His morning chores had changed not a whit in years, yet his father still delighted in supervising, as though his boy was too damn stupid to keep a thought in his head. Feeding the pigs was always the first order of the day, as they made the most godawful noises when forced to wait. Let the pigs go hungry a mite too long and the entire animal population falls into upheaval. Easing toward the sty, George kept an eye out for his father, who mainly kept to the shadows, popping out when George least expected it.

The wet slap of pig slop pouring into the trough covered the sound of his father's approach, but George's heart skipped a beat at the aroma of the pungent tobacco that always accompanied the man in the morning. The pigs went to work, their only job to gorge themselves and make for a tastier and more plentiful meal one day. George watched them, wondering if they'd eat his father as greedily as they devoured that slop.

"Glad to see you up with the sun, boy." Father's voice resembled an odd mixture of a grumble and a croak. "Your mama said you was havin' nightmares or some such bullshit."

"Yes, sir," said George. Putting aside last night's encounter, nightmares wasn't the right word, but any other answer might start a conversation George didn't particularly care to have.

A light rustle drifted down as his father sucked on the hand-rolled cigarette. "Too old to be havin' nightmares, you ask me. And surely too fuckin' old to be cryin' to your mama about it."

"Yes, sir." George gripped the wooden fence so hard his knuckles turned white. He fought the urge to spin around and glimpse the smirk his father undoubtedly wore. An exaggerated exhale filled the air around him with bitter smoke. A test. George held his breath to stifle any rogue coughing fits.

"A man what seen real horrors might revisit those things in his dreams every so often. But he learns to get up every mornin' and bury all that shit. Ain't no son a mine gon' be pissin' in his pants over a boogeyman. Hear me, boy?"

George squeezed the fence so tightly he half-expected to find fingerprints embedded in the wood later on. How much more pressure would he need if this were his father's throat and not some lifeless hunk of lumber?

"Yes, sir."

"Goddamn right."

The embers of the cigarette crackled softly as father took another hefty draw, then dropped it to the ground and stomped on it. A metallic clink made George's heart pound and the whooshing scrape of a leather belt pulled free from its confines confirmed his worst fears.

George squeezed his eyes shut, uttering a silent prayer for the leather strap and not the buckle this time. Surely nightmares didn't make for a bad enough transgression to merit the jagged metal wielded by his father like a medieval weapon. He held his breath, tensed his muscles, and waited for the first blow.

A joyless chuckle crept out of Father's mouth. This was all part of a cruel waiting game to drain fear from George before exacting the desired pound of flesh.

Bracing himself against the fence, George gritted his teeth and rocked back and forth, anticipating the harsh sting, almost craving the pain, just to get it done with. He would take his lashes and let his tears fall and then forget the shame when Merella knocked at his window that night. He opened his eyes at the thought of the lovely girl. The faint scent of cinnamon washed away the lingering odor of cigarette smoke. As if the very thought of her cleared his senses, George relinquished his grip on the fence and looked around in confusion.

He was alone.

If Janie Holcomb thought it odd that her little Georgie went from piss-your-pants scared of the woman at the window to accepting over the course of a day, she said nothing. Perhaps she suspected he'd been convinced to drop it. And with good reason. It wasn't often that George's father removed his belt and failed to employ it.

George watched her go about her tasks, stopping every so often and wincing as she rubbed her right shoulder. When she returned to her work, she favored her left hand a bit more than usual. George understood the cause, but kept his mouth shut. The aftermath of discipline wasn't something they ever talked about but seeing Mama like that only stoked the fire in George's belly. For now, he had it under control, but too much fuel and it threatened to escape its confines and set the world aflame.

The sunlight hours passed in a flash and George went to bed without a fuss. Maybe a little too early, because the kitchen candle shared its warm light for quite some time before Mama finally put it out. Merella said that light drew her to George's window, but he doubted she'd come to call with those flames flickering.

Darkness closed in, but George kept it at bay with hope. At first, anyway. The more time that passed without a gentle rap at the window, the deeper his heart sank. When it finally came, George sprung from the bed and nearly flew across the room. Merella greeted him with a subdued smile and shining eyes, then backed away so he could open the window.

George expected the window to creak, but it held its tongue. Clumsy as he was, he feared tumbling out the window and making a racket that would bring Mama running. Even if he escaped all that unscathed, Merella and he would undoubtedly run headlong into George's father, soused as the night is long, and nursing a mean streak wider than the Grand Canyon.

"Come and take my hand," she said, as he raised a leg to step out the window.

Butterflies fluttered in George's guts as he walked side by side, hand in hand, with Merella. Sweat coated his palm, while hers remained dry and cool as the Arizona night. She seemed perfectly content to travel in silence. Their footsteps scraping sand was the only accompaniment. After rejecting a bevy of opening lines, George settled on one.

"Where do you live?"

"I've lived all over. For the moment, here in Buzzard's Edge."

George's heart plummeted. "Where in town, I mean?" he asked, crossing his fingers it was somewhere nearby. He didn't think he could bear hearing her home lay in the center of the city, where the rich snobs would never let their lovely daughters mingle with an outskirter like him.

"If I told you that, George, what would you do? Walk me home?"

"I s'pose not. Just curious, is all. Don't your parents worry 'bout you?"

She smiled. "Don't yours?"

"Well, I don't suspect they know I'm out. Otherwise, I'd be in for a whuppin'." He forced a laugh, but Merella only narrowed her eyes.

"Sometimes I see your mother through the window. She looks kind. Tired, but gentle. I never see your daddy."

George stiffened, felt his chest go tight. It wasn't a question, but he still felt inclined to answer.

"Good."

Merella showed no trace of surprise. "Why?"

"He's just …" He studied Merella's eyes, hoping they'd tell him the follow-up was only her being polite, but curiosity lived in them. He sighed, then whispered, "He ain't good to us. Wouldn't be right to say much more than that."

Merella didn't answer. Instead, she studied George's face. A cold prickle climbed the back of his spine and he suspected she saw everything. Feared she *actually* saw everything.

When she broke her gaze, she said nothing, but placed her free hand over her lips and turned away. He followed her in silence, pulled in the direction of the still and unbroken horizon. George's eyes darted back and forth between Merella and the ground. He'd seen the girl disappear into nothingness the previous night and didn't plan on losing her ever again.

Wherever she was taking him, it wasn't her home. They wandered into the desert, past small sprigs of plant life riddled with thorns and hardy enough to survive the harsh daylight hours. The vermin had bedded down for the night and only the moon overhead accompanied them until they came to a lonely foothills palo verde tree, its branches reaching toward the sky in defiance of the unforgiving elements. A plume of life in the otherwise barren landscape. Merella donned a pleased smile and sat at its base, patting the ground next to her. George filled the spot.

"What do you think?" she asked.

The sand stretched endlessly in every direction, swallowed by the darkness at the edge of the moon's limits. George squinted in the direction of town, trying to make out the shadow of buildings.

"S'gorgeous," he said, turning his eyes back to her. "Uh, you come out here often?"

"When I can. People tend to avoid this place, but that's because they don't know what the dawn brings."

George paled and Merella laughed, a light and lovely sound. "Don't worry. We don't have to stay out until morning. Just a hint of sun and you'll see. We're at the perfect point, halfway between the town and the mountains. It feels like you're holding the two at bay, and yet, neither one can ever touch you."

The lovely words Merella strung together reminded him of Mama reading poetry aloud. An attempt to find beauty in the desolate landscape of their lives. George never could grasp what the poets were getting at but knew there was something bigger at play than the words themselves. George's heartbeat sped up again as Merella wrapped her cool, white fingers around his own. *Colder than the night air and whiter than milk.*

"What do you want to be, George Holcomb?"

His throat went dry and his mind blank. "A farmer," he said, the first answer that sprang to his mind. Then he shook his head.

"Think about it. Don't answer too quickly."

A moment passed, then another. George imagined the moon ferrying across the night sky, ticking away his time with this mysterious girl. Then the answer came to him.

"Free." Despite Merella's instruction, the word passed George's lips before his mind could wrench it back.

"Free," she repeated, almost tasting the word. "Are you not free now?"

His face reddened, and he hoped Merella hadn't noticed. He could only shake his head in reply.

She studied him. "Your daddy?"

George shifted uncomfortably. "Mama always taught me not to call him Daddy, but to call him Father. Even that might be too generous."

"What is he then?"

"A monster." His eyes wandered the coarse desert floor for a moment, then he raised them again. "Don't mean to be rude, but can we talk about something else?"

Merella shrugged. "Change nothing and nothing changes."

George nodded, but kept quiet for fear of slipping back into the same conversation.

"There," she said.

As if on cue, the vague, almost illustrated outline of Buzzard's Edge came starkly into view. Only with the shadowed buildings scattered like a child's toy blocks, did George realize how far they'd traveled. To the right and left, the land stretched toward an inevitable horizon. George had never seen the ocean but had heard stories about it and it seemed just as endless as this sandy sea. At their backs, the suggestion of sunlight peeked between the jagged tips of the Blackjack Mountains. They were titans, black shadows that loomed over George's world. They promised adventure and made his heart soar.

Merella saw only him. She conjured a coy smile. "I told you."

"Hot damn," he said, just above a whisper, the loudest volume he could summon.

"It never gets any less—"

She stopped suddenly, the smile drifting away from her lips and her eyes squinting as she jerked her head around.

George heard it too. Buzzing, almost like an approaching swarm of locusts. Sweat gathered on his brow and his stomach lurched. His mind barely had time to place the all-too-familiar alarm before two points of white heat sank into the back of his hand.

That wasn't buzzing.

A greenish-brown serpent pumped its venom into George's veins. The rattling intensified, emanating from a white-ringed tail that shook so violently it became a blur. Its task complete, the snake relinquished its grip, then shot across the sand as if the vengeful Old Testament God were hot on its trail. It vanished in the shadow of the mountains.

"Oh shit, oh shit, oh shit!" yelled George, holding onto his right wrist with his left hand. "It's swellin' up already. Don't it look bigger?"

Merella's gaze followed the snake, resting on the mountains and the dawn's light rising over their peaks.

"We have to get back. Maybe Doc Harrison can do somethin' but we gotta go!" Merella did not budge. "You listenin'?"

"It's too far," she said, absently. "That was a Mojave green, the worst one around here. White bands on the tail." She turned to meet his eyes with tears dancing at the edge of her own. "I'm sorry," she said.

"You're sorry?" he squeaked. George's eyes opened impossibly wide, and his breath came in short, desperate pants. "You mean—" He sucked in a wheezy breath. "I'm just goin' to have to die? That's all?"

She shook her head. "I didn't want to …" Merella left the sentence unfinished and huffed in impatience. "Take my hand."

George had not hesitated when Merella made the offer through the window, and in spite of his panic, he accepted once more. She gripped his swollen hand firmly, causing him to grimace. Her free hand sprang to life, not unlike the fleeing rattler, waving pale fingers in a boneless manner. Her intense gaze contained fire as her hand danced gracefully through the air. Tingles filled his inflamed hand, followed by a searing heat. The invisible fire caused more pain than Father had ever inflicted. George tried to jerk his hand away, but it remained locked in her grip. A ferocity took over her soft facial features and he questioned if he ever should have trusted her in the first place.

Merella's movements became more frantic, rapid and unpredictable. Tracers followed the swirling movement of her hand. Sweat trickled down the sides of her temples and George found himself paying more attention to her face than his hand. The sweet fragrance of cinnamon hung in the air and the agony, now spread throughout his body, bordered on unbearable.

With a final burst of wriggling, Merella thrust her hand skyward, and a flurry of amber liquid erupted from George's bulging hand. The yellow globules hung in the air just above their heads, maybe two dozen in all, glimmering under the first rays of the morning sunlight.

The venom, thought George.

The tiny pockets of liquid floated lazily as George watched. Perhaps more stunning than the view of the mountains. With a flick of her wrist, Merella conducted the bubbles like a symphony, as if picking particular notes from the air. The liquid danced in the morning light, certain death transformed into something dazzling and lively. With the song at its end, she whisked her free hand into the air and the venom careened into the sky, gone in a heartbeat.

"What are you?" George whispered, wincing at his indelicate phrasing.

Merella yanked her hand free and covered her face. Light sobbing sounds emanated from within. "Please don't ask it like that."

"I don't mean no harm by it. I … I think you're amazing."

"The hell you do. You think I'm a monster. You'll tell everyone and I'll have to find another home. Don't you lie to me, George. It'll only make all this harder."

"Hey now," said George. "I wouldn't lie to you. I don't think you're a monster, Miss Merella. Why, I think you might be just about the most beautiful piece of work God ever done put on this earth." A moment passed. "And I won't tell a soul what I saw."

A single bloodshot eye peeked from between her fingers.

"I mean it," he added.

"I see that."

"I hate to be so brisk, but that sun's peepin' over the horizon and I'm already goin' to catch hell, but if we hurry back, I might catch a little less." He smiled as if joking, though they both recognized the truth of the statement.

"Okay," she said, dropping her hands. "Okay. But is it alright if maybe we don't talk about what just happened?"

"Course. One condition, though. Will you come and visit me again tomorrow? Maybe we don't run so far away this time," he said, holding up his right hand, good as new, "but I sure would like to see you."

"I'd like that, George. Count on it."

George and Merella ambled across the packed sand, conversing in stolen glances and flickering smiles that said everything.

George hauled himself up to the window. As he lowered in silently, he turned to steal one more glance at Merella, but she was gone.

Magic, that one.

A throat cleared from the shadowy corner of his room and the stupid grin dropped from George's face. He hadn't thought to avoid trouble completely, but he hoped he'd get closer than this.

A twirl of smoke wandered into the light, trailing from one of his father's stinky hand-rolled cigarettes. The acrid smoke and the stench of whiskey overtook the room. George wondered how he'd missed it upon opening the window.

Like the devil himself hid that scent.

If he'd caught a whiff, he might have slammed the window shut and run off for better prospects. Hell, he'd take the snakes in those mountains over this. Then again, he knew he'd never leave Mama alone to deal with Father. Not much he could do now, but one day he knew he'd be big and mean enough to challenge his father.

That day wasn't today, though.

The curling smoke framed the gargantuan figure still hidden in shadow.

"Where was you, boy?"

George's head filled with buzzing—no, *rattling*, a muffled version of the snake's sudden warning.

"I'll say it again," said the gruff voice. "I been sittin' here for more'n a few hours and that bed's remained empty as the Lord's tomb on Easter Sunday. So, where the fuck you been?"

George remained silent, well aware the wrong words might change the severity of the discipline.

A low chuckle sounded, reminding George of boots stomping down a flight of stairs. When the laughter trailed off, a metallic *snikt* floated from the dark side of the room. Goosebumps rose on the back of George's neck at the familiar sound, and his blood turned to ice. The silhouette remained still, but George understood what his father was preparing for.

"You won't tell me straight out, I'll get it out of you the best way I know how. One thing sure as hell. You ain't gettin' out that window no more."

My God, what a world you love, George thought.

"Drop trou, boy, and get ready to repent."

That night, Janie Holcomb blew out the candle with a soft whoosh.

"Sleep tight, sweet thing," she said, but embarrassment crept into her voice.

Her light footsteps trailed off toward the kitchen, abandoning George to the pitch dark of his bedroom. Three muffled taps pecked at the windowpane. George balled his fists, wrapping them in the covers. Each tap sent a shiver up his spine. What was the point of walking over to her? George wasn't strong enough to pry loose the newly installed boards that covered his window.

Tap-tap-tap!

More urgent now.

He squeezed his eyes shut, wishing Merella would just pass by. Find another window.

"George?" She spoke softly, but the wood and glass didn't muffle the sound. He opened his eyes wide, coming face to face with the beautiful girl, only inches from his bed. Her sweet scent filled the room. He pulled the covers over his head.

"Did I do something wrong?"

George held his tongue, but trembled.

"No. God, no. Merella …" he started, but needed to say no more. He dragged himself out from under the covers.

A gentle light glowed in the palm of her hand. Not enough to draw attention from elsewhere in the house, but sufficient to illuminate the wide-eyed look of horror on her face. She covered her mouth with her free hand.

"What has he done to you?" she whispered.

George forced a smile but dropped it when he realized Merella didn't buy the false bravado. "Nothin' he ain't done a hundred times before. How … How are you doing that?" he asked, inclining his head toward the light sheathed within her hand.

She ignored the question and cradled George's bruised cheeks, staring into his blackened eyes as though she might find a deeper answer there. He had none to give.

"Don't s'pose you could fix me up again?" he asked.

She shook her head. "There's a sizable chasm between fear and hate. One I'm not yet sure how to cross. Hate leaves deeper scars."

George nodded, though he did not understand. He began to get out of bed, winced as his backside lit up in agony, and then pushed through to stand next to her. George stood bowlegged, as if having spent the day atop a mustang. When he opened his eyes from their squinting position, Merella's expression startled him.

Her eyes bugged from their sockets and her lips moved soundlessly. Somehow, she became paler. Although she looked at George, she appeared to stare through him and into the dark recesses of the unlit kitchen. A surge of adrenaline raced through his body as it went rigid, but the doorway remained empty.

"He won't ever let you grow," she whispered. "He'll kill you first."

"No." George studied his bare toes, unable to meet her gaze when he said it. "I mean, he lets me have it, sure enough, but deep down, he cares for me. For Mama." The longer George spoke, the less he believed his own words, and Merella appeared no more convinced than himself.

"It might be an accident, or at least look like one, but make no mistake, he will kill you." She eyed the dried crimson stain along his sheets. "George! No one who professes to love you would do such a thing." The shockingly stern tone demanded his attention. He looked up, saw the pain in her eyes.

A dark feeling rose inside George, bringing a bout of nausea with it. *Truth*, he thought. He'd always believed his father to be a good man, if a little detached, who got carried away when administering discipline.

Merella reached for his hand. "You said it yourself, he's a monster."

George took her hand and nodded slowly.

"And monsters don't stop being monsters if given time and enough slack on their lead. Monsters must be vanquished, or they will go on hurting, perhaps killing, indefinitely."

Tears gathered at the corners of George's eyes. "Can you stop him?"

The steel in her eyes subsided.

"You walked right through the dang wall in my bedroom. Course you can!" pleaded George. "You saved my life from that rattler. That was a monster, too."

"That snake was scared. It struck out of fear because we were in its home. Monsters seek trouble. They don't flee like a scared serpent."

"So what? What's the difference?"

"My power has limits. Boundaries, if you like. You'll need to be the one to fight your father."

"But … but I'm scared."

"There is no power I can summon quite as strong as one who has been wronged. One who seeks revenge."

"He's bigger'n me, though."

"And he knows it. Use that to your advantage. I can't fight him for you, George. But I *can* help."

He sat back on his bed, grimacing as his battered ass hit the mattress. "I'm listening."

"I'll need to think on it." She smirked. "I'm afraid I wasn't expecting this. It's not like I had a battle plan drawn up."

"Nah, I get it," said George. "You need to go to that tree, and sit a spell. I'll be alright here. Even if I could get out the house, I don't think I could hobble all the way there."

She stared at him for a moment as though he'd asked a question. "Can I show you something, George?"

"Of course." His heart fluttered.

"And you promise not to be scared?"

"Hell, I promise to try."

She pulled her hand away and closed her eyes, then began moving her hands through the air the way she had done to heal George earlier. Faster and faster until her fingers seemed to multiply in a frantic blur. The hardwood floor shifted to a lighter hue. The cracks between slats vanished as the knots in the wood swirled to become whirlpools of sand.

George's eyes wandered the room. The ceiling gave way to a star-filled night sky and the walls vanished, leaving behind only open air. The shadows that perpetually lived in George's room took on the shapes of the Blackjack Mountains. The cool night air brushed against his cheeks, and he knew if he shifted his gaze ever so slightly, he would see Merella's tree, but he only turned enough to see her.

Concentration filled her eyes as she summoned the scene into existence. The hint of a smile lit her face as she snuck a peek at George, and the moon became his boarded-up window once more. Her grin faltered, and she turned her attention back to the mountains. Her own version of freedom.

George felt the sand between his toes, felt the cold desert breeze ruffle his hair. And then it was gone. The rough wooden floorboards returned beneath his feet and Merella collapsed on his bed, her breathing labored and her hands still.

"Did you really take us out there?" he whispered.

She shook her head. "I can make people see things. Play on emotions. Joy and fear are the easiest to work with."

"Wow."

She interlocked her hands in front of her. "You're not frightened?"

"Not even a little. Merella, I don't think you could ever hurt me."

Worry creased her face, but it was gone in a second. "I have to go."

"But you'll be back tomorrow? And we'll figure all this out?"

She nodded and helped George into bed, then lightly kissed the corner of his mouth. Backing away, she wriggled her fingers and disappeared into the shadows.

For the first time all day, George's backside didn't bother him. He was floating.

George lay awake for hours after Merella left, afraid his father would arrive home further in his cups than ever and ready to unleash hell. His heavy eyelids betrayed him before long and if his father arrived with his usual ceremonial ruckus, George did not stir at the cacophony.

That morning, George beat the sun to rising. He fixed himself a small breakfast, quiet as possible, so as not to wake Mama before her time. A hopeful air helped him push through the razor-sharp pain that jolted through every step as he made his way outside.

The still morning air lacked that low, sludgy voice that reveled in correcting mistakes, real or imagined. George tensed his shoulders, expecting his father to appear around each and every corner.

Maybe it finally happened. Maybe the bastard drank himself to death.

George allowed himself a hint of relief at the thought, but dismissed it just as quickly. It was too easy. When a knight arrived to fight a dragon, he never found the dragon dead in the cave, having choked on a cow bone. No, monsters required slaying.

If the world took care of them in the first place, George wouldn't have spent his first eleven years living in fear.

An odor caught George's attention outside the pigsty, freezing him in place. Not just the usual shit stink the pigs gave off in spades, but an accompanying offense that stung the nostrils.

Whiskey.

A reek that clung to his father like hair to a tarantula, and it wafted from inside the sty. Darkness claimed the contents within as the rising sun had yet to reach that far.

George inched closer to the dim sty and peered around the corner, fearing one of his father's cruel tricks. The man lay sprawled in a haystack, naked to the waist and surrounded by his own sick. His breeches hung open, revealing a nest of pubic hair strangling his penis.

Bile rose in George's throat and for a moment, he thought the man might be dead after all.

Then his eyes shot open, bloodshot and haunted. They saw through George for a moment, lost in the blinding sun, before focusing all their rage on the boy. Father grumbled something unintelligible as he clambered to his feet, yanking his pants up to cover his shame. The belt hung from his right hand, wrapped around his palm with the buckle reflecting the sun's light in warning. Once on his feet, Father swayed back and forth as if debating what to do with his son, having wandered in on him like Ham stumbling upon the nakedness of Noah.

George froze for a moment, waiting for his discipline, watching the shimmering buckle swing lazily by his father's feet. The gleam captured George's attention, drawing his gaze to the second pair of feet jutting out from under the hay pile. Cold in their appearance and devoid of color. George recognized them immediately.

"What did you do to her?" George asked, ice in his voice.

"Huh?" His father stepped from the shadow, squinting stupidly. When his mammoth body no longer blocked the view, George saw his Mother splayed on the floor, clothes torn to expose her ravaged body in a way he'd never wished to see. Dark purple bruising wrapped around her neck in the fashion of a noose, distracting George from her sightless eyes for only a moment.

The story unraveled. Father returning from the saloon at an ungodly hour. Mama trying to keep him from George's room, leading him away from the house. Their all-too familiar, if not quite consensual, routine grew out of hand, and this was the result. And the fucking bastard didn't even remember doing it.

A voice spoke from the back of George's mind. *Change nothing and nothing changes.*

He threw himself at his father, easily outweighed, but not letting it slow him down. Father raised an elbow to stave off George's attack, knocking the boy to the ground with a dull thud. Dust flew up around him, begging him to stay down. Play dead. But anger clouded George's better judgment. He burst from a prone position, scratching and biting at exposed skin. The salty taste of blood filled his mouth and his father let loose a primitive bellow, not unlike a branded cow. George wrenched his head from side to side, trying to cause as much damage as possible until an open palm the size of a pig's head blindsided him across the face and returned him to the ground from whence he came.

George spat and felt a tooth pass through his lips. Before he could throw himself at his father once more, the man raised his right arm and slung the belt down with a mighty force. It slashed through George's shirt and tore into his chest. He wailed as he tried to cover the open wound with both hands. Eyes squeezed shut, George heard the whoosh of the belt before it cleaved into his bicep, slicing through skin and ripping down to the muscle. George screamed his throat raw. He rolled around as if trying to put a fire out and his arm burned as he felt the buckle tear free.

George lifted his trembling hands to cover his face, afraid the next blow might strike there, but after a moment of thrashing and writhing, nothing happened. Risking a peek, he surveyed his father standing over him, stock still and so wide-eyed, George thought he might've been privy to the Lord's return. Sweat poured from the massive man's brow and the front of his pants had gone dark with foul-smelling piss.

"What the fuck?" George rolled to safety and came to rest against the feet of Merella. Her black shawl brought with it the essence of night even in full daylight, emphasizing her pale white skin. She held her left hand perfectly still while carving intricate designs into the air itself with her right.

She kept her gaze fixed on the dumbfounded form of George's father, locking him in some sort of manic daydream. An illusion.

George wasted no time getting up. A quick scan for weapons revealed nothing until his eyes lit on the belt dangling at his father's side. George's blood still trickled off the pointed buckle. He closed the distance in a single large step and unwrapped the belt from his father's outstretched fingers. As he hoisted himself up the man's mountainous shoulders, he caught another look at his mother's prostrate form. Murdered by the man who'd vowed to love her, cherish her, take care of her until death parted them.

Rage rekindled in George's eyes as he wrapped the belt around his father's neck, cinching the loop, and dropping to the ground to draw it tight. Whatever fear Merella had planted in the man's mind kept him upright. Even as his eyes darkened, the expression of unbridled terror never left. Not until the light dimmed from them completely. George watched the spark vanish an instant before the behemoth's legs gave out and he toppled to the ground. Even then, George planted his feet against the corpse and continued yanking the belt tight—screaming, cursing, and crying for his life.

Merella dropped the hex and sank to her knees, exhausted. She couldn't even bring herself to comfort George. Still bleeding, he sobbed uncontrollably as he continued tugging on the belt. A moment later, strength deserted him and Merella regained her feet and sauntered over.

"Come and take my hand," she said to the mess of a boy lying in a pile of dirt and blood.

Tongues of flame swallowed the stables and barn, then they began to lick at the house. Eventually, they would consume everything on this soon-to-be uninhabited spit of land. The animals, what few the Holcomb family kept, bleated and squealed as George herded them off in the direction of the closest farm. Most would make it there and lead a rich, full life. At least until someone required a slab of bacon. Some would get picked off by coyotes, but that was just the way of the world.

My God, what a world you love.

When the animals had started on their journey, a lone black foal lingered behind.

"Probably need a horse," he said, grinning at Merella.

"What the hell? Bring him along," she replied.

Hand-in-hand, he set off with Merella toward those beautiful mountains as the midnight-black horse trotted behind them. Buzzard's Edge held nothing for him. Never had, if he was honest. The only part worth staying for was his mother, and she was gone now. He looked over his shoulder as they started out for the open desert and his heart leaped as the flames grew higher.

"I like to think that's Mama, keeping that flickering flame going one last time to keep the darkness away," he said softly.

Merella squeezed his hand and smiled.

"I wanted to ask you." George looked away. "What'd you make him see at the end there?"

She bit her lip and thought for a beat. "Everyone has a monster."

Her icy blue eyes put the period on that sentence. He didn't need to know anymore. George nodded. "What'll we do next?"

"Oh Georgie, I've gotten by for a long time on my own. We're resilient, you and I. We might have to steal every once in a while, but we'll do just fine."

"Yeah," he said. "Yeah, I reckon you're right."

The mountains loomed in the distance even as the silhouette of the town disappeared against the horizon. George didn't recall the peaks being so far away the last time they were out here.

THE REAPING, PART III

"I like that one better," says Josiah. "Something like love wins out, and the monster gets his in the end."

Vulture tilts its head to the side. "Do you say so?"

"Well, sure." He frowns. "What other way is there to take it?"

"As just the start of a different story," says Coyote. "The birth of a monster."

"I don't follow." Josiah squeezes the hatchet, for comfort. *My protection. My burden.*

When his eyes flit between the animals once more, he sees something on their faces. Judgment, perhaps. Certainly an awareness of the weapon he carries, its honed blade.

"We should move on," he whispers. "What else do you have to show me? Stories to tell? Other souls in this godforsaken land?"

"Whoa, there," says Coyote. "That's an awful lot of questions for one breath. As far as what else to show?" It glances toward Vulture. "Ain't much to see for that last story, nor the next, except what lies outside the town proper. Middle of nowhere, just about. Not unlike where we found you. That's where they both happen."

"You mean 'happened'?"

Coyote says nothing, only pants in a way that resembles a grin.

"What about your story?" asks Vulture. "Surely a man who finds himself in the middle of the desert with nothing but a blood-stained blade must have a thrilling tale to tell."

Josiah shakes his head and lowers his eyes. "Traveling west in a group of four. My wife, Annabelle, and a couple friends. Ezekiel and Esther. Made it to within a couple hundred miles of where I met you all. Then we spotted a horde of Apache. Followed us two days before they snuck up in the night. Slaughtered everybody."

"Everyone but you," says Coyote. Not a question.

Josiah bounces the hatchet in his hand, the blade so dull and blood-browned, there isn't a single spot to reflect glares of sunlight. "If it wasn't for this thing, I'd have joined them in the afterlife."

"You killed them all?" asks Vulture.

"The Apache?" Josiah swallows hard. "I hacked at them that were close enough—might've got one or two—then managed to run off and into a patch of woods. Climbed a tree and stayed still as petrified wood 'til the sun came up."

"Sure is lucky they gave up on you," says Coyote.

"Lucky's one word for it," says Josiah, narrowing his eyes.

"Forgive me sayin' it, but you don't seem that broken up for losin' your wife."

Josiah kicks at the sand. "Yeah, well, we all mourn in our own ways, don't we? I had a lot of time while I was walking, to think and scream at whatever passes for God out here."

Vulture flutters down from the schoolhouse steps. "Come, we'll head toward the next notable location."

Josiah twists his eyebrows into a knot of concern. "Thought you said the next tale happened outside town."

"That it does, Josiah Dennis. But there are still many stories to tell, and some of them occur right here in the heart of Buzzard's Edge." Vulture looks toward Coyote. "Perhaps you remember the story of Elijah Sparrow and Renny? I'd like to take to the sky and scout our destination while you tell it."

Coyote assents with a quick howl. "I do like this one. 'Bout a guilty conscience, it is."

"Don't give away the ending." Vulture wrinkles its bald head into a scowl, then its eyes go wide. "Dear me, where are my manners?"

The bird fires into the air, circling once, then vanishing over the top of a nearby building. Before Josiah can say a word to Coyote, Vulture returns with a pocket mouse dangling from its beak—limp with its tiny head hanging at an unnatural angle—and holds the small carcass out toward Josiah. As he takes it, he notes the pointed edge of Vulture's beak.

"Not much meat on it, I'm afraid, but it should settle your stomach while you listen." The glint in Vulture's good eye suggests he would be wise to accept the offering.

Hand trembling, Josiah brings the mouse to his lips, sinks his teeth into the small body, and feels a trickle of warm blood run across his tongue. He nearly gags as the bristly hairs tickle his throat but manages to force the meal down.

The taste is bitter, but it's been so long since he's eaten.

HOLES

Like everyone else in Buzzard's Edge, Johnny Mabry heard the tales about the new sheriff. Elijah "Hellfire" Sparrow. Typical of this shitty little place. Building up a myth around its newest lawman to scare off the brigands who'd previously declared open season on the town.

Yeah, Johnny Mabry knew the stories and wrote them off as bullshit, until the moment he sat tied to a stake outside the town, hands knotted behind his back with Elijah Sparrow staring down at him. The sheriff aimed a Colt pistol not at Johnny's head, but at the ground next to him. A line of coal-black gunpowder slithered out from underneath the notorious outlaw like a rattlesnake fleeing across the scalding desert. The sand was hot enough under Johnny's ass that the gunpowder might take mind to go up on its own.

"What you want from me?" Johnny choked the words out through a sob. Death often plagued his mind, yet he had hoped he would meet it with more gumption than this.

"Want you the fuck outta my town." Elijah stared at his gun. Didn't deign to meet the eyes of the man begging for his life.

"Fine. Cut me loose. I'll ride west and you'll never see me again, I swear it!"

"Not good enough." Elijah took a few steps back. He knelt at the end of the sleek, dark line of gunpowder and lowered his pistol. With a deafening bang, the trail of gunpowder sparked, blazing to life and racing toward its intended.

Johnny had no time to cry out before the dynamite packed tightly under his ass blew him to smithereens, raining chunks of Mabry from the sky. Shit, some of him maybe even landed back in Buzzard's Edge. Only on the outskirts, though. That was alright. The bloody precipitation wouldn't bother the people who paid Sparrow's salary.

The first hole appeared outside of Elijah Sparrow's cabin, no bigger around than a silver dollar. What it lacked in width, it seemed to make up in depth, far more than just an indentation. Although that was only a guess. He didn't hold any great desire to go sticking his fingers down there to verify. When Jeb first sniffed out the hole, Elijah cursed the mangy mutt away from it. Last thing he needed was a snakebit dog collapsing on his land. Lord only knew where that beast had got off to now.

With the vinegar gone from his lips, Elijah softened a bit, guilt bubbling to the surface. Dumb as a post the dog might be, and half coyote to boot, but Jeb remained his sole companion after the town of Buzzard's Edge abandoned him. Or he abandoned them. Depended on the vantage point you chose.

Elijah. A whisper, riding on the breeze, catching him by surprise.

"What you lookin' at, Mr. Sparrow?" The voice asking was light but with enough husk to carry and always contained a smile.

Goddamn. Was it Tuesday already?

Renny strode across the sand, wearing little more than the groceries that hung by her sides and just enough cloth to cover her unmentionables. She visited old Elijah once a week, however, and being spotted in that state of dress had never proved a problem before. The land surrounding the desolate cottage gave way to harsh conditions and flat plains as far as the eye could see, encouraging any self-respecting towns person to steer clear.

"Ain't nothin'," Elijah spat through his droopy mustache. Tobacco had tinged his facial hair an unsightly shade of yellow, not far off from piss. He turned his back on the hole to study Renny from head to toe, hoping she wouldn't try too hard to peer around him. Something about the little tunnel to nowhere made the hair on his neck prickle. He couldn't nail down what exactly, but the hole seemed too dark for daytime.

By God, she looks beautiful today, Elijah thought, as he drank her visage up.

Her legs stretched out so long, surveying them made Elijah's eyes tired by the time they reached her thighs. A great set of tits lay hidden underneath a swathe of cloth that barely passed for a shirt; big enough to give a man a handful, but not so boisterous they might cause a woman to lose her balance. Although Elijah's eyes lingered on her body, it was Renny's face he most looked forward to during these visits. Warm, kind eyes and a genuine smile that bespoke that old hooker with a heart of gold cliché, all underneath an untidy mop of brown hair that some men might call too short, but Elijah thought suited her to perfection.

She raised an eyebrow in a playful gesture as she drew closer. "Just outside inspecting the dirt then, is that it?" Renny climbed to her tiptoes, struggling to see around the former sheriff, but she wasn't tall enough to get a good look.

"Just a hole some vermin dug. Never you mind," he said, but made no move to reveal it. Elijah knew her buying that weak excuse was every bit as likely as getting a horse to waltz, so he quickly changed the subject.

"What you bring me?" He gestured at the canvas bags dangling from Renny's long fingers.

The girl shrugged. The bag clinked and sloshed, providing the only answer Elijah needed. "Nothin' special. Just a couple items from McGregor's to tide you over a while."

The same exchange every week, like a dance; Renny playing coy and Elijah eagerly anticipating the next step.

She held the bag out, eyes still searching the ground that stretched out behind Sparrow, the mysterious nature of his yard a long way from forgotten. "Where's Jeb?"

Elijah scratched the back of his neck and looked around. Renny nearly made him forget the dog's existence. "Run off somewhere, I guess. He'll be back. Always is." He took the bag and dug through his pockets, fishing out a few silver dollars that called to mind the size and shape of the hole. Dropping the coins into Renny's outstretched hand, he mumbled something about keeping the change. Only after the girl made the money disappear did he realize he didn't know one way or another how far a dollar would fare in a general store these days.

Renny offered a half-hearted grin, her face not betraying the answer to Elijah's unasked question.

"Like to come in?" Elijah's cheeks reddened in a way unbecoming of his Hellfire days. One of these times, she would say no, and he didn't think he could stomach that.

"Love to, Mr. Sparrow."

"Elijah, please," he said, heeding her smile. The embarrassment written on his features had not escaped her notice.

He tried not to think too hard on it. Best to let sleeping dogs lie. Speaking of sleeping dogs, he scanned the deserted yard once more, listening carefully for any sign of Jeb's whereabouts, but the land remained silent. Not so much as a whisper.

As Elijah turned to go inside, a pinprick of darkness caught his eye. Another hole. Unease clenched his stomach as he realized, even at a distance, this one would have housed a silver dollar with room to spare.

Place is overrun by pests. Got us an … an infestation, he thought, detecting a tremor even in his internal speech. He followed Renny in and slammed the door behind him; a clamor that he expected must have echoed all the way to the nearest neighbor.

Renny's clothes dropped to the floor. There she stood, naked as the day she was born, and in his parlor, no less. Her head low, as if searching for the confidence that usually came with putting oneself on display, but she wore an inviting smile. Elijah wondered what he'd done to deserve such a bounty. The thought quickly fled from his head alongside the blood flow needed elsewhere.

The groceries hit the floor with another clink, muffled this time, and he approached her lithe form, unbuttoning his shirt as he crossed the room. Renny retreated, an impish look plain upon her face as she led him to the bedroom. He found her there, splayed upon the mattress, eager and ready for him. Once she bit down on her lower lip, Elijah's pants struggled to contain him any longer.

It had been a long time since he'd fucked a woman without paying for it and if the notion of foreplay had ever existed within his mind, it was buried somewhere in the back now. Prostitutes never kissed, but he believed if Renny were to allow any man's lips to grace hers, he'd be the one. A mischievous twinkle made his heart jump as he gazed into her eyes and trailed a weathered hand up and down her body. Her pale white skin, never tanned even under the Arizona sun, felt smooth as the finest China silk. She gasped at his touch, reaching up and unbuttoning his pants.

Unable to wait any longer, he plunged inside her. Warmth consumed him, gripping tighter with every thrust. As Elijah bucked away, taking care to find something resembling a rhythm, Renny dug her nails into his back, tracing the scars earned from previous battles. Elijah grimaced at the pain.

He closed his eyes as he drove himself into her, lost in her cries and moans.

BANG!

A gunshot split the head of Anderson Downs, an accused cattle thief who would never stand trial. The top of his skull vanished, as if part of a magic act, while flaps of skin draped down in a pathetic attempt to hide the damage. His body stood for nearly five seconds before receiving the message that it was dead and should, therefore, make acquaintance with the ground.

Sweat gathered on Elijah's brow as he tried to shake the image.

Jeffrey Livingstone pleaded for his life, tears lining his puffy red eyes. "I've stuck up my first and last bank," he cried, right before Elijah drove a serrated knife into his stomach, ripping the lining to shreds and spilling reddish gray coils of innards among the sand, unnaturally bright against the dull desert.

In and out went the knife. In and out.

Renny's passionate cries mingled with the screams in Elijah's head—frequent visitors he alone was doomed to hear. On the first occurrence, he'd gone soft as a foal's down and apologized profusely. Since then, he managed to push through it, extracting as much joy as the meager bit of life left to him would allow.

Faith Dunn stared over his shoulder, ice in her eyes, as her body rocked back and forth beneath his. The woman felt no remorse for drowning her babies in the bathtub, so why should he feel shame for delivering comeuppance? Justice. He stole her last remaining bit of warmth and then filled her with his seed, before leaving her bound in the middle of the desert as the night grew cold.

Elijah opened his eyes as he climaxed and terror wrapped cold tendrils around his heart as he met the dead eyes of Faith Dunn, imposed upon Renny's face. She pulled him tight as the final spasms took hold, a convulsive death grip to prevent his escape. Relief only set in as Renny's face returned to its sweet, comforting normal.

He rolled to the side, wiping himself off with a crusty sheet. Renny shot him a concerned look, but didn't allow it to dally. The two lay in bed, their labored breathing the only sound. Their tryst hadn't lasted any longer than a man like Elijah—not yet old, but prematurely aged—could maintain, yet the sunlight streaming in the bedroom window had changed positions, sinking a little further toward the horizon.

"Guess I'd better get back to town," said Renny, without making a move.

"Yeah, I guess you better." Elijah's voice was distant. His eyes remained fixed on the ceiling, studying something that wasn't there. Somewhere beneath the bed, a scratch sounded against the floorboards. So faint, it was easy to ignore.

The silver dollars clinked together as Renny stepped out on Elijah's porch in the cooling desert air, walking with an unsteady gait. He appeared almost comatose as she abandoned him, but she expected he'd be situated with a glass of whiskey in his dank, disheveled parlor by the time her feet met the sand.

The former sheriff of Buzzard's Edge wasn't much to look at, wasted away after having spent the past few years drinking himself into oblivion, but he still radiated a sense of power. If pressed, Renny expected that was why she still made a weekly trip out to the middle of nowhere to throw him a fuck. Some misplaced sense of adoration and puppy love. That and he paid well. So well, in fact, she suspected all those rumors of corruption and violence that followed the name of Sparrow like flies after a hearse wagon must hold some water.

"Necessary evil," she whispered as she got her bearings and squinted in the direction of Buzzard's Edge. That's what the people said about him. He cleaned the muck off the town's boots that his predecessor was too afraid to touch. It was only after Sparrow's single failure that the murmurs began about how terrible he'd been. When he made every attempt to execute a local hellion known as Noose Holcomb, and inexplicably failed in his duties because the outlaw refused to up and die at the end of a hangman's rope.

She might be the only person who knew that when Sparrow fled west, he hadn't actually left the town's borders.

Caught in a reverie with a grin on her face, Renny hadn't taken a single step away from Elijah's porch. Something else niggled at the back of her mind. He'd blocked her view when she arrived. But what had been hiding?

The sun dropped lower every minute, yet still provided enough light to study the ground. At first, Renny saw nothing, thinking the old man had finally lost it, then she noticed the holes in the ground. A multitude of them, no less than twenty, and all large enough to catch a man's ankle and give it a nasty sprain. Renny fell to her knees, placing her hands against the sand that still held the sun's heat. It stung her palms as she stared into the closest hole.

An odd, shimmering blackness returned her gaze. Renny's stomach took a tumble as her brain attempted to translate what she saw; the darkness one anticipates inside a small tunnel, but only because that's what she expected. The blackness covering the top of this hole appeared as though something had placed a cap over the crevice, shielding the viewer from the horrors contained within.

Renny reached out a hand to touch it, positive the darkness would have substance, then jerked it away before making contact. Probably not a wise idea to plunge her hand into the unknown. A whisper reached her ears. Renny stood straight up as though a freezing cold hand had goosed her backside.

Not a whisper. Whispers.

Voices held a certain quality when they talked about a person, rather than to them. These murmurs issued from every conceivable direction—above, below, behind, and even right in front of Renny's dumbstruck face, as absurd as that notion was. The mixture was so muddled, Renny couldn't decipher a single word as the susurrus continued to condescend. Each syllable sounded familiar, as though if she were able to focus on just one voice, the meaning would become clear. But that didn't happen. Renny grew red in the face, going from frightened to pissed off in the space of a heartbeat. She opened her mouth to scream in frustration when an ungodly pain chomped down on her foot.

The scream turned into a quick yowl. Tar-like blackness seeped from the hole, wrapping Renny's foot in an icy embrace. Freezing cold needles stabbed by the thousands and each one hit a nerve, piercing tendon and flesh.

Renny squeezed her eyes shut, forcing tears from the corners and gritting her teeth so hard she expected one to shatter. She screamed once more, but it offered no relief. When she tried to look down, she knew what she would see before her eyes took it in. The substance had sucked her leg in up to the knee, not climbing so much as yanking her into the depths. The frozen shards of pain returned as she simultaneously heard and felt a bone snap in her leg.

"Elijah!" Her voice was little more than a mewling squeal, not even powerful enough to reach the house a stone's throw away. Sparrow might not be able to stop what was happening, but he could try, goddammit!

Renny's right leg sank to the crotch as talons severed the flesh from her inner thighs. Razor-sharp claws sliced into her pelvis and for the first time, she felt thankful she couldn't see what was happening within the murk. Her left leg, perched on the ground away from the miniature abyss, rose at an unnatural angle. Tendons pulled and popped when they reached their limit, and her ankle ascended over her head. The hole gave no quarter, sucking Renny's stomach, then chest, into the pit. It hadn't been large enough to accommodate her body at first, but ribs snapped, and internal organs shifted to new shapes and locations as Renny disappeared little by little.

When all that was left above ground was her head and neck, she wondered how much of her still existed in some capacity. Freezing cold fire ate at her extremities and shards of broken bone poked into the soft parts of her body, but her mind retained a perfect clarity even as she wished to black out. Some otherworldly force wanted her to experience her own end. Twenty-two years old and this was as far as she'd get. Frigid hands closed around Renny's throat and just when she thought she had found the strength to scream once more, she went under.

Though Renny knew no more, she felt everything.

Elijah had a drink fixed less than a minute after Renny walked out. Wasn't no mixing to the way he took his liquor. Pick up the bottle and serve. How the fuck else were you gonna forget all the bullshit that cycled through your head when you were trying to know a woman in a biblical sense?

The remaining liquid sloshed noisily against the sides of the glass bottle as Elijah half sat, half fell into his favorite chair. Maybe not the most comfortable, but it suited him fine. He breathed deep and heavy, staring fixedly at the wall, when a howl broke his concentration. Some damn coyote or something. Or maybe Jeb returned. He perked up at the thought but remained lodged in the wicker chair. Despite pretending to be cross with the mangy beast earlier, he hoped Jeb was okay. In truth, he always looked forward to the dog's company. Renny's too, though any interaction from townsfolk that didn't end with him being called a murderer or a coward—two very different sides of the coin—was okay with him.

As if reading his thoughts, the gold sheriff star on the table caught a passing glance of light. Almost as if to say, *I remember the times, Sheriff Sparrow.*

Hellfire.

I remember what those ungrateful motherfuckers choose to forget.

He sank deeper into the chair, reveling in the lingering scent Renny had left on him. Love wasn't the best word to describe what they had, but it didn't entirely miss the mark, either. At least from his point of view.

Elijah, a voice whispered, causing him to stiffen and eschew any notes of drunkenness he had accumulated in the last few minutes.

The drab hollow of a parlor remained as devoid of life as ever. Nothing moved, not even a flicker of shadow. He raised the bottle again, shaking his head as he brought it to his lips and took a generous pull. Liquid fire to drown out the unnecessary noise the world provided, whether you wanted it or not.

Skrit, skrit, skrit.

Three sharp staccatos burst under his feet, soft but unmistakable. Something trying to claw its way out.

Rats, he reasoned, not believing his own bullshit for a moment. Rodents abounded in the desert, but Elijah had inhabited this cabin for some years and never had to contend with vermin moving freely under the floorboards in the past. Placing the bottle down with uncharacteristic tenderness, he eased to the floor and placed one ear against the wood. The blood pounding in his ears reverberated against the dusty boards and the groans his body produced roared in the comparable silence.

Maybe he'd imagined the scratches. A foolish grin formed at the corner of his mouth. Then the sound came again. More frantic this time, the scratches sent Elijah scattering. His arms failed to save him from landing on his ass. He scrambled away from the source of the noise, but it followed, slinking beneath the house.

A light rumble shook the floorboards, and Elijah pictured a monstrous serpent writhing through the sand. Cold sweat gathered on his forehead, quickly spreading to the rest of his body and unleashing the acrid stink of fear. It overwhelmed any remaining aroma that Renny had left behind. Squeezing himself into a corner as a means of retreat, Elijah's heart pounded. Scratches closed in on his position, tearing at the underside of the house. The monster's urgency crescendoed, resonating through the walls until it surrounded him. Elijah cupped his hands over his ears, but it did no good. The floor trembled beneath his feet, nearly knocking him over again.

Sparrow.

Whatever beast thirsted for his blood. *They* had sent it.

Faith Dunn, Anderson Downs, Jeffrey Livingstone, Johnny Mabry, and the others. So many others.

Their names bolted through his bedraggled mind, his put-upon mind, at the speed of light, creating a desperate whirlwind of whispers and clawing. The tempo increased. The beast below was almost through. Shoddy flooring could not hold its fury at bay much longer.

Then, at once, it stopped. It all stopped. The noise, the names, the movement. The cozy, isolated cabin on the outskirts of Buzzard's Edge regained a sense of tranquility. Elijah slid down the wall and cradled his head in his hands. He was tired all of a sudden, so very tired.

A new noise caught his ear, but not one to make his heart beat clear out of his chest this time. A small yelp, distant, but within reach. It echoed from beneath the floor as though traveling through a long-forgotten series of caves.

"Jeb." Delight crept into Elijah's voice. Of course, the dog wound up under the floorboards. A chuckle escaped his lips at the insane notion of a great scaly beast traversing the sands underneath him to exact some sort of revenge. What had McGregor topped the bottle off with to make him believe such nonsense?

He pulled himself to his feet and plucked a wool coat off the back of the chair to go and search for his companion. Throwing open the front door, the first thing Elijah noticed was how quickly the sun had dropped. A line of brightest orange spilled enough light to make up for the lack of the moon's glow, caught halfway between day and night. The second thing he noticed stole every bit of confidence from Elijah.

The holes covered his yard, dozens of them. Some no larger around than the first—*a silver dollar*—some massive enough to devour a horse. Elijah stood still as a cactus on a calm day, studying the new landscape. The darkness within each hole undulated against the light, but absorbed that beautiful orange, rather than reflecting it.

Elijah, a voice whispered. No. Voices.

It sounded as though every hole spoke. A variety of timbres combined to create a symphony of the damned. High, low, loud, soft, and every imaginable interval between, chattered in a ghastly unison that forced the hair on his arms to stand at attention.

"You *have* come for me, then," said Elijah, unable to keep from trembling.

"Not you." To his left, the darkness filling one of the craters formed the dead-eyed, hateful face of Faith Dunn. It spoke in her familiar dull tone, stating facts without emotion. Taunts filled the air, stemming from each and every trench that now honeycombed the landscape of Elijah's yard. The words cut like a freshly stropped blade before joining together in a convoluted chorus. The voices seemed to speak in an unknown tongue, something equal parts ancient and terrible.

"Wouldn't dream of ending your suffering, Sparrow." The playful tone belonged to a man. It stood out crisp and clear against the muddled chants.

Elijah tore his gaze from the Faith-hole to see a gaunt, fish-white hand emerge from one of the larger pits, clawing at the surrounding sand. Painstakingly, the hand dragged itself forth, the body of Johnny Mabry attached to the other end. When Elijah last saw Johnny, a concussive explosion blew him to so many bits, he couldn't fill the stomach of a vulture. The ghoul clambered to its feet, not so much an image of the man before, as an unholy mass of skin stitched back together by the type of magic men feared. The kind of dark magic that had saved Noose Holcomb from the hangman's rope and cost Elijah Sparrow his dignity.

Mabry stood to his full height, his patchwork body creaking as he moved, even when his lips pulled into a hellish grin. The choir sank to a dull roar.

Mabry tipped his hat, loosing a few maggots. Elijah watched them scurry across the hard-packed sand and squirm into the roiling dark they'd ridden in from.

"Like the lady said, we ain't here for you, Elijah. Not here to kill you, anyway."

"Then why did you come? Just to put a fright in me?" He spat on the ground, tasting bile as it left his lips, and summoned more bluster than he thought possible. "It won't work."

"Here for vengeance, Mr. Sparrow." Mabry grinned, letting the words hang.

The cold sweat returned as confusion set in.

"Elijah," called a voice, more fear than malice in its tone. He recognized it immediately and his heart missed a beat.

"Renny," he whispered.

It called again, twice more, softer each time. It might've called a third time, or that could have been the wind breathing across the plain. As he strained to listen, he thought he heard a dog bark in the distance. It didn't come from under the house this time.

"Hellfire, they called you," said Mabry, staring at the tears as they cut through the grime on Sparrow's cheeks. "You know nothing of hellfire, sir. Surely you will someday, but death would be too easy, too quick, for the likes of you."

"If not kill me, what do you aim to do?" Any trace of fire in Elijah's words had disappeared with Renny's pleas. His pathetic whispers could not have crossed a silent room.

"We aim to cut you off. Seal you up in this hovel like a tomb and make sure you spend every miserable fucking second alone. Anyone or anything who tries to give you comfort will know pain and suffering the likes of which words cannot do justice." He paused, as if expecting a retort from Sparrow. He received none. "She loved you, you know. I expect you'll have to live with that. With your sins."

Once again, Mabry found only silence in the cool desert air. He filled them with his parting words. "Remember Sheriff, we'll always be with you. Every flicker of the wind, every inexplicable bad feeling, every scratch at the floor ..."

Mabry seemed poised to continue, but instead kept mum, his eyes fixed on Elijah. A bubbling, black oil-like substance enveloped his pale visage. Tendrils wrapped around him lovingly and drew him back toward the dark hole. The menagerie of voices diminished to nothingness, as one-by-one the holes contracted until they ceased to exist altogether. Less than a moment after standing face to face with a man he'd blown to smithereens, Elijah watched the land return to its familiar appearance. The last vestige of sunlight dropped below the horizon, and coarse sand shone under the emerging moonlight.

With the last of his strength drained, Elijah Sparrow fell to his knees. The stream of tears coursed down his face like a mighty river. His chest hitched, whether for Renny, the dog, or the future, he couldn't rightly say.

A touch of whiskey might help ease the hurt, but he needed to conserve his stores. Lord only knew if—or when—he'd be able to leave this place again.

THE REAPING, PART IV

With a bead of sweat dripping down his forehead, Josiah spies the sand at his feet. Not a single hole or imperfection to be found. The realization does little to calm his nerves.

Vulture cuts through the air with a carefree swoosh, landing atop a building constructed out of wood so fresh it could've resided inside a tree only days earlier.

"Well, we're here," says Coyote, sitting on its haunches and gazing at Josiah expectantly.

"Where's here?" Josiah asks, as he stops before the rugged structure, stepping into Vulture's shadow. The darkness should cool the sweat gathered at his temples, but somehow it feels hotter inside the gloom.

Tink.

Tink.

Tink.

Vulture's beak taps at a sturdy set of iron bars.

This is a prison, he thinks, heart racing. Then he notices the stain beneath the bars, swathed across the side of the building in a rusty maroon that matches his weapon.

"Don't rain much out here," says Coyote, "though what little we get never seems to wash away the blood."

"The sand devours it with greed, but the stains never quite fade from man-made items." Vulture narrows its eyes. "There is almost an intentionality to it. Wouldn't you say, Coyote?"

"I might at that. Some might even say, a warning."

"A warning. I like that."

Josiah's head spins. The taste of blood still lives on his tongue and a stray hair tickles the back of his throat. "Warning against what?"

The two animals trade a glance. Coyote lifts a paw as if to say, "All yours."

Vulture emits a guttural noise, like a man clearing his throat before he gives a speech, only not the same. Not quite natural.

"This next story—"

"No!" cries Josiah, raising the hatchet. "A warning against what?"

Quick as a stray bullet, Coyote bares his teeth. Razor-sharp canines peeking from behind dark lips. A growl rumbles in its chest, never bubbling to the surface, but making its presence felt, nonetheless.

Vulture's body tenses, a spring ready to uncoil at a moment's notice.

Careful, thinks Josiah. *They may be intelligent, but these are beasts at heart.*

Slowly, Josiah lowers the hatchet. It dangles by his side as he calculates his odds, imagines Vulture's keen beak piercing his eyeball even as he buries his hatchet in Coyote. Imagines Coyote's teeth tearing out his throat as he lashes out toward Vulture.

Josiah swallows a lump in his throat.

I am a prisoner.

My eternal reward. My torture.

"The next story." The words dribble out of Josiah's mouth, weak as the urine stream of a dying man.

Coyote and Vulture stare for another moment, then hide their teeth and relax their posture, respectively.

"The next story," continues Vulture, voice smooth as a pond on a calm day, "takes place on the other side of those bars. It also takes place in those mountains that loom on the horizon and even begins far east of here. A civilization so civilized it drives out good men and killers alike."

"Will you hear it?" asks Coyote, just above a whisper.

Will I? Josiah wonders.

WHERE THE DAYBREAK ENDS

Tink.

Tink.

Tink.

The imprisoned man tapped a long fingernail against the bars of his cell, the only sound he'd made since the sheriff hauled him in.

"Don't s'pose I could convince you to knock that shit off?" Billy Chambers leaned back in his chair and kicked his feet up on the desk, making sure his deputy badge remained visible at all times. He stroked his scraggly beard as he considered the man in the cage. Boy might be a little closer to the truth.

A pause, for the briefest of moments.

Tink.

Tink.

Tink.

Billy hauled his feet off the desk and stood so quickly he sent the chair clattering to the ground. "Now you listen here and listen well, mister." Billy poked a long scarecrow-like finger in the prisoner's direction. "This town don't take kindly to kidnappers and murderers roamin' our borders like they own the place. Ain't about to put up with your shit in here, neither."

The tapping stopped.

"Kidnappers." Bathed in shadow as the boy was, Billy didn't see his lips move, but the voice held more weight than someone so young should be able to lift.

"What one man calls kidnapping," the boy continued, "others might call love."

Billy approached the cell. "Stranger, those is two words that don't belong in the same sentence. Ain't a soul in Buzzard's Edge considers what went on between you and that other fella love." Billy spat. "Arguin' the point'll find you at the end of a noose. And that's if you're lucky."

The prisoner cleared his throat and stepped out of the shadows.

"If you plan to hang me, I won't put up a fight. Everything I have to live for is gone, anyway. Stolen. But at least do me the honor of calling me by my name."

Sheriff Harden had thrown the prisoner into the cell, slammed the door, and then stormed off grumbling, leaving Billy to hold down the fort and without so much as a name to call the captive by.

The stranger grasped the bars in a way that suggested he could bend them if he wanted, but instead chose to allow his imprisonment. A light scruff dotted his pale cheeks, and his eyes held the same heaviness as his voice. *Haunted* was the word that galloped through Billy's head.

Billy sneered, but it was a put-on and he suspected the stranger knew it. "Alright, let's have it, then."

"My name is Wes Bradley, but if there's only one name you remember after they commit me to the ground, I hope it'll be Andrew Martin."

"That the man who—"

"Deputy, if you want to hear my story, I'm happy to tell it, but I won't tolerate interruptions."

The sadness living in the stranger's words gave way to an authority that would have cowed Wild Bill Hickock himself. Billy eyed the man's knuckles, thinking about giving them a solid whack to show who was boss. Then he smirked, realizing he kind of wanted to hear the kid's story.

"Alright then, Mr. Bradley." Billy picked up the chair and plopped himself down, crossing his arms and returning his feet to the top of Sheriff Harden's desk. "I ain't got nothin' but time and I'm always up for a good yarn."

"This one hasn't got a happy ending, Deputy."

Billy nodded and Wes Bradley told his tale.

The first thing you need to know is Andrew's eyes are like black holes. A very slight ring of gray surrounds those endless pits, and when I looked into them for the first time, I had to grab hold of something to keep from falling in. His knowing smile told me I wasn't alone.

Andrew and I quickly became inseparable, albeit discreetly so. Even brushing his fingers when we passed felt like courting trouble from the Massachusetts elite. A new country that in many ways failed to escape the issues that plagued the old one.

Any New England man worth his salt knew the quotes from Leviticus, from Romans, that forbid one man from lying with another. Vague words twisted by hard-headed men. In Andrew, I knew a kindred spirit, but we grew tired of meeting under cover of darkness and seeking each other's warmth in the cold shadows. We longed for more.

Don't get me wrong, neither of us anticipated the new frontier would welcome us with open arms and embrace our love. But we hoped the untamed land and its sporadic population would leave us alone.

Strange how things work out.

Our nightly excursions took on new life—from stealing kisses to stealing supplies. Andrew's family was prosperous. One of the main reasons he could never tell his father—a man who slept with a Bible under his pillow and a rod by his nightstand—that courting a wife held no interest. For as strict and cold as Mr. Samuel Martin was, he had every reason to fear the community would ostracize him for his inability to shepherd a godly son.

We gathered enough stores for two months as well as money and hunting supplies, aware that the journey may exceed our design and trading posts would be in short supply. Then we held our breath, suddenly sure that fire and brimstone would rain down in the form of an intervention from Mr. Martin or his friend and confidant, Mr. Weeks—the man who lived alone on a hill at the edge of town. Mr. Weeks drew rumors of magic and mysticism from the lips of the townspeople; a peculiar friendship for the penitent Mr. Martin to uphold, but one he defended, nonetheless.

I have not yet mentioned my own parents, as they are both a blessing and a curse. A blessing because they would not have raised an eyebrow at who I chose to love or what I did with my life. A curse for the same reason.

The night arrived and we fled town at the devil's hour. Andrew exhibited a natural inclination toward tracking and navigating—ideas which, to this day, still confound me. Perhaps it was related to the stars in his eyes. He set our course, and silence filled the streets, excepting the infrequent nickers and light slap of hooves as two of Mr. Martin's horses pulled the stolen wagon southwest toward our destiny.

I hesitate to mention our departure's lone strange occurrence, but given the bumps and bobs our story was to encounter, it seems prudent. With civilization swallowed by the darkness at our backs, and only trees and fields ahead, we saw no living creatures, neither man nor beast. Except for a pair of eyes, watching from the woods. They floated above the ground, too high to belong to any beast. Not such an awful sight except for their haunting green glow—illuminating the night in a manner that rivaled the moon—and the intelligence that lived inside them.

A hideous idea arose within me, churning my already unsettled stomach. The mind behind those eyes knew our plans and would inform anyone in town who would listen. Perhaps the eyes belonged to the mysterious Mr. Weeks, himself. An odd and upsetting notion. Choosing to keep the terrible sight to myself, I gave Andrew a peck on the cheek and received a smile suited to those endless eyes. I snuck one more glance back, but the darkness had swallowed those green orbs. I relaxed as much as I could, but the sensation of being watched never quite deserted me.

In the early days of the trip, we rarely stopped, afraid to allow any pursuers time to catch up with us. When we discussed this aloud, we referred to parents and pastors, but the emerald eyes had seared themselves into my memory.

I will not bore you with a day-by-day account of our entire trip, but with a week under our wheels, we began stopping to rest, usually sleeping in shifts, only relaxing our guard to make love on occasion. In those moments, the paranoia disappeared, if only for a short time. Being able to hold each other close without fear of reprisal was the reason for the trip, after all.

At various intervals along our journey, the watchful eyes reappeared, and I could no longer keep them a secret. Always far away enough for Andrew to convince me it was a trick of the light, but with a degree of cunning in their shine that kept me from believing him. Still, I agreed. If only because his face appeared uneasy. We told the lies to comfort each other.

"Don't you think we've gone far enough?" I asked every few days, but Andrew always shook his head, donned a spirited grin, and answered the same way. "The more distance between Massachusetts and where we put down roots, the less time we'll need to spend looking east and waiting for trouble to find us. We can focus on where the daybreak ends." He smiled. "Our new home."

Where the daybreak ended was Arizona. The lush supply of endless water and game dried up along with the landscape. The preserved food in the back of the wagon had lasted longer than anticipated. A boon, because the desert provided little addition to our stores.

You may have the impression that Andrew made the majority of the decisions, and you would be correct, but determining where we'd settle, where the daybreak ended, so to speak, was my responsibility. It was the Blackjack Mountains that made my mind up, cutting through the flat land like a saw through rotted wood. Laced with green in an otherwise tan and desolate landscape. Beauty among the ashes.

A town called Buzzard's Edge rested across a sandy plain, a ways from the slightest incline. Far enough to grant us the solitude and privacy we desired, but within reach of a monthly trip for food and anything else we might require. We agreed it best we didn't travel into town together, lest we find the locals displayed a New England level of understanding and suspicion. A couple hours a month spent pretending was a far cry from wearing that mask every second of every day.

While most people would still call the mountains barren, they offered up enough life to feel like home. Maybe even enough for the bow and arrow we'd packed to be of use. We set to building a cabin over the next few weeks, and while Andrew had almost single-handedly gotten us to our destination, the construction was my specialty. Seeking out and selecting the proper wood for a long-lasting structure came naturally to me. It was a two-person job, but I took great pleasure in designing a home to keep our heads dry. Assuming it ever rained out there, that was.

A reasonable supply of preserved food had survived our trip, packed away in jars beneath crates of clothing and a hideous serape Andrew had insisted upon buying in the Twin Territories. Still, we needed fresh additions to our stores if we were to avoid scurvy.

The first trip to the town of Buzzard's Edge rested on Andrew's shoulders. Once he set foot in their general store, the job would belong to him. A mysterious hermit living in the mountains, stopping by for fresh food and the occasional piece of hardware. People would believe that. Naturally friendly, Andrew's biggest problem might be refraining from being overly talkative, but if it meant our safety, I believed he could do it.

As the sun peeked over the tops of the mountains, Andrew saddled up one of the horses to the empty wagon and set off toward town, leaving me to place some floorboards. Every nail I drove in resonated through the hills, emphasizing a loneliness that could only exist in this uninhabited country. It struck me that I could scream at the top of my lungs, and it likely wouldn't reach a soul, a truth that simultaneously thrilled and terrified me.

For more than an hour, I meticulously placed and attached the long wooden planks that would serve as the foundation for our home until thirst pulled me away from the job at hand. The midday sun beat down, subtly burning my bare chest and shoulders. Unrelenting brightness and sparse shade left no place to hide, yet I felt the familiar sensation of being watched.

Would those terrible green eyes that chased us from Massachusetts even show up in the daylight?

I wiped sweat from my brow and studied the surroundings, watching for any sign of movement. Sparse trees dotted the hillside, more life than the desert at the base of the mountain promised, but with the exception of a few fluttering branches, nothing moved. I shook my head and gulped from my water skin. Paranoia stemming from dehydration and the ceaseless Arizona heat, no doubt. Nonetheless, my eyes skimmed the tree line as I drank.

A flash of green bathed the skeleton of our cabin in moss-colored light. An accompanying buzz blared through the atmosphere. I spit out a mouthful of water and dropped to the ground. A legion of insects—wasps, locusts, the most vile of God's creations with wings, all closing in on me. That was the only possible explanation for the sound. Except the skies remained clear, the sun unblemished.

The green light continued to pulse, a flickering candle with an unhealthy pallor. My heart raced as I spotted the source. A stone's throw into the woods, a plank-sized gash tore open in the afternoon air, a murky darkness buried behind the sinister glow. My eyes widened as I crawled behind a woodpile, studying the newfound curiosity and searching my mind for possibilities. It remained obstinately blank.

The buzzing that resembled an approaching horde of gnashing insects intensified. Something was going to come through that hole, and it was going to come soon. As if reading my mind, a disembodied hand burst from the opening. When I tell you the hand was dark, I do not mean it belonged to someone of African descent. Measuring the tone of this being's skin against the night sky would be like comparing the ebony and ivory keys of a piano.

The massive hand drew its owner forth, the body smooth and featureless. A white haze, tinged with the faintest hint of blue, surrounded it, only visible when it stepped out of the sun. The horrid screeching whir emanated from this cursed creature. I imagined its flawless midnight-black skin packed to capacity with bugs; pinching, biting, and clamoring for their freedom.

Although it had no vestige of a nose, the figure raised its head to sniff at the air. Sweat gathered on my upper lip and I held my breath.

It was hunting.

Making as little noise as possible, I rolled underneath the frame of the cabin, thankful I'd laid enough boards to shield myself from both the sun and this insidious creature.

Dirt and pebbles rained down through the slats as the creature stepped into the space that would become our parlor. It crossed to the kitchen, then Andrew's study. Footsteps augmented by the almost mechanical whir of the demonic beast. Nausea gripped my stomach at this violation. Incomplete as our home might be, the otherworldly being had invaded it without a care.

A worse thought suddenly took hold. Andrew. He had been gone most of the morning. What if he returned to find this *thing* occupying our house? How could he hope to fight off a being of pure darkness?

Tears formed at the corners of my eyes, and I clapped a hand over my mouth to stifle any rogue sounds. I refrained from even breathing as its footsteps transgressed the floor above. Perhaps a minute passed, perhaps an hour, before the creature gave up the structure as deserted and hopped down to the dirt. A cloud of dust rose in its wake, filtering through the slats and threatening to trigger a sneeze. Painfully, I withheld the urge.

I eased my head around to peer through a gap in the wood and watched it wander into the trees, taking the incessant humming with it. The glowing green hole in the world—the same color as the eyes that chased us across the country—floated a foot or two above the earth, awaiting the return of its resident. It welcomed the shadowy intruder before shrinking away into nothingness with a light snapping sound.

I sucked in small breaths, careful not to make too much noise in case it was a ruse, but something inside told me the thing was gone. I felt its absence. Isolation and solitude returned to the woods, and I welcomed them.

When Andrew returned, he found me sitting at the edge of the newly laid flooring, but the neatness with which the boards were set clashed with my current state. Covered in dirt and grime, tear stains running down my cheeks, and an unnatural shake about me that just wouldn't quit.

"It's my daddy's friend. The man on the hill," he said, after I'd told my tale. "It has to be."

The reaction surprised me, given his hesitancy to believe anything less than natural could be in pursuit of our wagon. I told him so.

Andrew squeezed my hand. He didn't apologize, at least not with his words, but his tone held enough regret for two. "Everybody in town is scared of him. You must have realized that, Wes. He built that house five, six years ago, but the construction never stops. Shovels smacking rock, hammers hitting nails, at all hours of the night. My mother said once they must be digging a tunnel to hell. Daddy didn't like that. He shot her a nasty look, and she spent the rest of the meal studying the contents of her plate."

"How could it be that man, though? Mr. Weeks, isn't it?"

"My mother didn't just mention that tunnel to the underworld off the cuff. There's all kinds of rumblings that Weeks is into a world of funny business. Comes into town and everybody, but everybody, is afraid of him. Why, you remember that boy that went missing back last summer?"

"Of course," I said. "Not every day a kid goes missing. Besides, I went to school with the sister. Hempel."

"Benjamin Hempel," said Andrew. "And they never did find him. There's more than one or two folks that say Weeks was behind it, that he takes kids." He looked down and kicked at some stray rocks. "More than one reason I was anxious to leave that place behind. Wes, what if my daddy employed his help to find me? Find us."

My eyes widened. "I'd say that's far-fetched, but you weren't here. I've never seen anything like that before, and I sure hope I never do again."

Silence overtook the air. I can't speak for Andrew, but my brain was kicking up a dust storm in search of more reasonable solutions.

"Maybe it's coincidence. Some kind of creature that only lives in the wilds this side of the country." Andrew's face contained so much hope that it broke my heart to shake my head.

"I just can't forget the green eyes, Andrew. This thing didn't stumble across us. It knew where to look, where to … appear. I wonder if it had found me, if it would have dragged me through that odd tunnel. Maybe brought me back to your daddy."

Andrew caught my gaze, and I remembered the first time I'd ever gotten lost in his eyes. "Wes, I'd rather be dead than go back."

I nodded. "I'd rather die than lose you." I whispered the words, but found I meant every syllable.

Camping out under the stars lacked some of its original appeal after the shadow incident, and we aimed to finish the cabin as quickly as two able-bodied men could. We made good time, but I don't mind sharing that we probably could have shaved off a day or two if I wasn't so intent on listening for that phantom buzz.

If my theory was correct, and that awful creature was hunting us, why hadn't it returned?

I'd almost forgotten about it by the time the roof went up. Andrew and I spent most nights on the floor of the bedroom, only blankets between our bodies and the unforgiving floorboards while the night stars peered down at us, but once the final piece went into place, separating us from those stars, the pile of lumber became a home. We still needed a bed to christen, but that would come with time. For now, it was enough that in the rare event of rain, we would remain dry.

That afternoon, we celebrated by carving our initials by the door.

A.M.

W.B.

When the sun came up the morning after we placed the final board, Andrew lay next to me, scratching his head. "Running low on supplies again, Wes." The implication was in his words and the nerves that pervaded his tone. What he really meant was *I have to leave you again.* He hadn't forgotten about the shadow creature.

"Let me go for you. Or better yet, let me come with you. I'll hide in the back. No one'll even know I'm there."

He smiled and shook his head, then leaned over and kissed me on the neck. "Not worth the risk. Hide, if you like. Lay low, but I bet nothing shows up to bother you."

I raised an eyebrow at his confidence but came up short on arguments. He was right. Up here, worst-case scenario was me hiding under the sheets for a couple hours. Down in Buzzard's Edge, it was both of us getting labeled as sodomites and potentially lynched.

My head hummed with arguments, but none were worth the effort to spit out. Besides, I didn't like the idea of Andrew leaving under less-than-positive circumstances. I get the sense he felt the same way. He dressed in a hurry as I jotted down the necessary items. When the list was complete, I tucked it into the pocket of his vest, forced a smile onto my face, and kissed him goodbye.

The front door shut with the gentle brush of wood breezing by wood. I congratulated myself on the craftsmanship but didn't care to linger anywhere near the entryway. Andrew's footsteps padded through the brush and to the wagon. A soft nicker carried through the trees and found me inside, still sitting upright in our makeshift bed; too concerned about stirring the shadows to move, but too tired to properly hide. Andrew understood this state of paralysis and had assigned me no chores in his absence.

The morning passed in relative silence, though every time a light breeze rustled the branches outside, I stiffened and my eyes went wide. The occasional whir of a nearby paper wasp set my teeth on edge. I waited for it to either fly away or join in with a thousand of its brethren, voices harmonizing together in darkness, hunting.

But the sound passed, and eventually the sun climbed overhead; a surefire sign that Andrew would return soon.

As if spurred on by that thought, the hint of snapping twigs and wheels churning the dirt made their way to my ears, promising safety. For the first time in hours, I tossed the blankets aside and rose to my feet, stopping at the window to see if I could catch a glimpse of Andrew through the sparse flora and fauna.

He burst from the tree line, face as white as the sheet I'd unceremoniously let fall to the floor. His mouth hung open as he dashed for the cabin. I raced him to the front door and threw it open. His arms were empty of supplies. I never did find out whether or not he had finished the shopping.

"The eyes," he said, and my stomach plummeted to my feet. I stared over his shoulder, expecting the cunning glare of those green orbs or the emergence of the shadow creature. The sight that emerged from the woods terrified me considerably more.

Andrew's father, Samuel Martin. All the way from Massachusetts and standing there in the flesh.

Two men flanked his side. The first wore a long-sleeve cotton shirt, too hot for this weather, and a black Stetson. He carried a pistol that caught the scant bit of sunshine cutting through the canopy, making me wish we possessed something more formidable than our fists, a bow, and questionable aim. The second man wore a gold star that reflected as brightly as the first man's firearm. He carried a single-barrel rifle and a scowl that appeared just as friendly.

At a glance from Mr. Martin, the two armed men, who I presumed to be the law of Buzzard's Edge, stopped at the border of the clearing, fingers resting a breath away from the triggers.

"Thank the Lord you're safe." Andrew's father held out his arms in anticipation of an embrace. "I prayed nightly that I might arrive before this *demon* could harm a hair on your head. He hasn't hurt you, has he, boy?"

Andrew's eyes iced over like a New England pond in January. "How did you find us?" His words lilted up at the end, but it wasn't a question so much as an accusation. A low buzz sounded, thin and lonely, like a single wasp trying to find its way back to the nest.

Mr. Martin's welcoming grin faltered. "A little help from a friend."

"The kind of help that your Lord might frown upon, I wonder," said Andrew. "You hypocrite."

The two lawmen raised their eyebrows at the impertinence but obeyed the request from Mr. Martin.

The rasping of insect wings grew closer and more dense, no longer a single wasp. A bead of sweat dripped down Mr. Martin's temple. "Now, I don't believe that's for either of us to say. I thought you'd be grateful to Mr. Weeks, agreeing to use his… influence to help me find you, get you home to your mother. Rescue you from that"—he inclined his head toward me—"heathen." Seething with rage, I stepped forward, but Martin's harsh growl caught me off guard. "Do not move another muscle, young man, or I will order those officers to put you down like the dog you are."

I raised my hands in surrender.

Andrew shook his head. "If half of what I've heard about Mr. Weeks is true, he's not a friend, and you never should have trusted him."

"That's enough backtalk out of you, Andrew," snarled Mr. Martin. "Now, get away from that devil."

Through clenched teeth, I said, "I don't know what you think—" The buzzing surged, and my eyes darted around the clearing, searching for the source, waiting for the sky to open and unleash those shadowy figures. Except for the dissonance combing through the air, the afternoon remained tranquil.

Mr. Martin shook his head. "And I don't know what kind of abominable notions you put into my Andrew's head, Wes Bradley, but I intend to drag you both back to Massachusetts, where you will stand trial for kidnapping and attempted sodomy." He squinted his eyes and the crescendo of his voice climbed over the thunderous slapping of wings.

I wanted nothing more than to clap my hands over my ears, but he didn't appear to be bluffing about ordering the officers to shoot. Both law men had lowered their weapons slightly as their puzzled eyes searched for the source of the sound.

"And if I find out that you forced your carnal urges on him, well—" Mr. Martin froze with his mouth hanging open, a sudden ill pallor overtaking his face. A green glow emanated from the base of his shirt collar. Samuel Martin barely had time to peer down and locate the source of his discomfort before a solid hand the color of obsidian shot from his chest, tearing free from cloth and flesh and spraying a mist of blood across the man's face. Martin's eyes widened in shock before the rage abandoned them alongside any spark of life.

A second arm thrust outward, followed by the chiseled body of the phantom. It emerged from the husk of Andrew's father, ripping the man in half and littering the clearing floor with blood and bone.

A chilling shriek cut through the hollow. Whether the appearance of the creature or the evisceration of his father caused Andrew to bellow, I never found out. The cry called the law men to action. They raised their weapons and made them spit fire at the shadow creature, but the bullets had no effect. Each round simply passed through the phantom as though it weren't there. I dove to the ground to avoid the stray shots.

"Andrew!" I reached out for him, but he remained frozen, eyes crawling over the scattered remains of his father. When he had surveyed every last inch of the battlefield, his gaze found me, and life rekindled in his eyes. He didn't quite smile—that would have been too grotesque for words—but there was love. There was also sorrow. Like he knew.

"Andrew!" I screamed so loud my throat burned.

An emerald-tinged opening floated in the air where Mr. Martin had stood only moments ago. A desolate murk roiled inside the window to another world. The pitch-dark beast from within that hellscape bolted at Andrew with terrifying speed. I tried to crawl to him, grab hold, but it made no difference. The phantom wrapped a brawny coal-black arm around his chest and wrenched him into the gaping chasm. Andrew's screams persisted until the knothole in the air closed to the size of a frying pan. The last thing I saw as it diminished to nothingness was Andrew's eyes. The first bit of him I ever took in, as endless as the Atlantic Ocean. Those same gray eyes stared back at me, pleading for help. They vanished from existence with a barely audible snap that extinguished the remnants of the insectile swarm and the wails of agony.

Then, the afternoon grew silent, my voice capable of screaming no longer.

Sometime near the midpoint of the story, Billy had lowered his boots from the sheriff's desk and sat forward like the most attentive pupil in class. When it became clear Wes was finished, he waited a moment, staring in wide-eyed awe, before speaking out.

"Well, wait a minute. That can't be the end, though."

Wes shrugged. "Takes the story up to about an hour before I arrived here. Those two men—I never did catch their names—rushed over after Andrew disappeared, trudged through the messy remains of Mr. Martin, and hauled me to my feet, shouting about how I killed two men. Utter foolishness. I had no weapons. Besides, even from their vantage point, one man had exploded, and the other vanished into thin, dark air."

Billy stared down at the desk, like he might find some answers engraved there. "What'd they say on the ride back?"

"Not a thing. And probably for the same reason they hightailed it out of here and left you in charge. I feel for them, I do, because I've been in their shoes. They have no idea how to come to terms with what they saw. So they threw all the blame at the closest scapegoat. I don't care for it, but I understand it."

"We seen some things 'round here, that's for sure. A witch, a man that bullets couldn't touch and nooses couldn't kill, but what you're describing?" Billy shuddered. "I don't understand you, Mr. Bradley. They're goin' to hang you and it sure as shit sounds like you didn't do nothin' wrong."

Wes chuckled. "Well, I've got you on my side, at least. What would you say if I asked you to let me out? I could even black your eye, convince them I escaped all on my own."

"Well, I … uh—"

Wes laughed again, but there was no joy in it. "Yeah, that's what I thought. Don't worry, I'm not asking. They can do what they want to me. I've got nothing to go back to. My stars are gone."

"Last time you saw Andrew, you said he was alive. Ain't that some kind of thing worth hopin' for?"

"He might not be dead," said Wes, hanging his head, "but he's gone. And I suspect that might be worse. Truth is, every time the sun sets from here on out, and the sky goes black and fills with stars, I won't be able to think about anything else. It'll carve out a hollow in my chest until I can't feel anything at all. Deputy, I think I'd rather go while I still have something to hold on to. I just hope wherever I end up, they don't have anything near as awful as that phantom."

"I'm mighty sorry," was all Billy could say. His voice sounded tight.

"I appreciate that." Wes ambled to the far side of the cramped cell, staring out the window where the sun acquainted itself with the horizon, just past the Buzzard's Edge gallows. "Andrew would have said that's where the daybreak ends."

Billy nodded.

As the two men waited for the sheriff to return, they sat in silence, broken only by the occasional rap on the metal bars of Wes's cell.

Tink.

Tink.

Tink.

THE REAPING, PART V

"Christ, that one gets me," says Coyote. It swipes a paw at its face, as if drying a tear away.

"Certainly not the town's proudest moment," says Vulture.

"That … phantom." Josiah's eyes dart around, as if expecting a green haze to open up in the middle of the street. "Are they plentiful in this area?"

Coyote's tongue lolls out the side of its mouth. The aggression from only a short time ago is gone. Temporarily, at least. "There's an awful lot of unexplained, maybe questionable, things in these here parts, Mr. Dennis. Lot of 'em is just monsters in human skin, though."

"What my friend means to say," says Vulture, "is no, that ghastly phantom is not usual. A creature like that never graced the region before, nor ever again, after the taking of Andrew Martin."

"You got a strange way of talking," says Josiah. "Like a man who can look in all directions at once."

Vulture preens its feathers as though in response to Josiah's words.

"I guess you probably got more places to take me, more stories to tell." He kicks at a puff of sand, then freezes, foot hovering inches from the ground. When he speaks, he tries to inject a firmness into his tone. "Say, I appreciate the drink, the food, and the wisdom, but what's our destination?"

"A few more stops, another yarn or four," says Coyote, "and I'd say we'll be just about ready to meet everybody."

Josiah raises his eyebrows, swings his head side to side as if he might find a crowd around him. "Everybody?"

"Yes sir." Coyote stands and nips at Josiah's sleeve. Gentle, as if leading the man, but once his coat is in the beast's grip, the pull is unrelenting. Josiah has no choice but to follow.

"The citizens of Buzzard's Edge, of course." The featherless pink skin on Vulture's face pulls back in the twisted bastardization of a smile.

"Well, let's go, then." As he speaks, Josiah hears the nerves in his own voice. Even with the ever-present threat of the creatures at his side, he considers throwing the hatchet away. The muscles in his right shoulder twitch, ready to toss it where no man will ever touch it again. Before he can act, reason stays his arm.

My only protection, my burden.

Vulture soars overhead as Coyote leads Josiah away from the prison.

"So, where's the next story take us?" asks Josiah.

"Well, we're headed to a special shop, but the tale that happens there is still a little ways off," says Coyote. "Next story I got for you begins at the railroad tracks."

Josiah skids to a stop, a hopeful warmth kindling in his chest. "There is a railroad in town? This is wonderful news!"

Coyote's eyes flick toward the sky as Vulture's shadow drapes over Josiah. "Well, don't get too excited now. Sure, Buzzard's Edge'll have a railroad, and someday there's gonna be a body rottin' right on the tracks."

Josiah narrows his eyes, the confusion addling his mind keeps any words from emerging.

"Thing is," says Coyote. "It just ain't been built yet."

TRADE SECRETS

The train screeched to a stop, jostling the passengers around me from their stupors. Murmurs drifted from every direction. At first, I mistook the noise for the general excitement of having reached our destination, but the wavering tone that accompanies worry grabbed hold of my attention. I jolted forward and leaned toward the window. An ocean of sand flowed toward the horizon, a landscape unlike any seen back east. A thing of beauty, if not for the stunning lack of civilization.

We had arrived early, but not at Buzzard's Edge.

"Why are we stopped in the middle of the goddamn desert?" grumbled a surly voice.

Alarmed mumbling quickly grew to a dull roar, and the engineer made no appearance to assuage his passengers. The panic intensified as men passed outside the windows. One in the lead and two more a few paces back. Despite the knocks and shouts from my fellow travelers, the strangers outside paid no attention, only kept moving toward the front of the train. The crescendo of voices made picking out individual words and phrases difficult, and fear hung heavy in the atmosphere. Likely the masses believed we were being boarded, robbed, but a man such as myself who has worked with law men all over this great country recognizes authority when he sees it. An air of confidence in their stride and six-shooters at their hip worked in tandem with a gleam at their chest to mark them as officers of the law.

Embracing my opportunity, I plucked my satchel from the floor, then pushed through the stifling crowd to reach the nearest exit. The officers gathered outside the train, their faces pale as winter snow. Dear me, but this couldn't bode well. The glass tinked softly as I rapped my knuckles against it. Of the three men, only one turned his head. Thankfully, that proved sufficient.

As I said, law recognizes its match.

When the officer approached and the passengers realized the door would be opened, the pressure grew at my back, but the man who opened the door drew a massive revolver and held it aloft. "This here's a crime scene," he bellowed. "Get back to your seats and we'll have you on your way fast as we can."

He gave me an inquisitive look as I slipped out the cracked door, dropping to the hard-packed sand below.

"How long's that gonna be, Harden?" shouted a gruff man from inside the train, the same voice that had criticized the conductor's point of cessation. He wore a wide-brimmed black hat and a gaudy red sash tied prominently around his waist.

"Hell of a lot faster if you shut your fuckin' mouth, Fowler!" The officer turned back to me, revealing his badge with the word "Sheriff" emblazoned across the front. He cocked his head and donned a sheepish grin as if to apologize for the language. "And who might you be?"

"Thaddeus Locke," I said, offering a hand. "Full-time educator, part-time consulting detective."

"Consulting detective?" He raised an eyebrow. "Shit, that's a new one to me, but I s'pose we could use all the help we can get. John Harden, by the way." He didn't raise his hand in return. Nor did he holster the revolver. "Well, Mr. Locke, you don't dress much like an Arizona man. All that black, the sun woulda gobbled you up long ago. Where you from, hoss?"

I cleared my throat. "All over, really, but most recently, Cambridge. It's right outside of—"

"Boston. I heard of it, though I can't rightly recall where. And what brings you out here from Cambridge?"

"I'm traveling to Buzzard's Edge for, shall we say, a change of scenery. May I ask why you opened the door to me while keeping the rest of the cattle hostage?"

Harden snickered. "Cattle, huh? Maybe you'll fit in here after all. In answer to your question, I guess I just got a good feelin' about you. Dressed real spiffy too. S'pose you just look like a man who knows his business." He studied me for a moment before continuing. "Detective you may be, but I sincerely doubt you ever seen nothin' like this. Murder, and a real nasty one at that. You sure you want to come along, Mr. Locke?"

"I think you might be surprised at what I've seen, Mr. Harden. If you'd like to point me toward the body, I would be honored to be of service, if I may?"

Harden smirked. "Oh, the guys're gonna love you. Right this way."

Steam billowed from the stalled engine's smokestack, hissing and putting a scare into the three horses held by a tall gentleman who sported a salt and pepper beard with a scowl behind it.

"This here's Virgil Morgan," said Harden, "and the other fella goes by Jeremiah. Boys, this is Thaddeus Locke. Says he's a consulting detective and wants to lend a hand."

Morgan acknowledged my existence with a series of grunts. Thin as a rail and with a fine coat of peach fuzz about his cheeks, Jeremiah nodded as he fiddled impatiently with a Bowie knife. I shuddered as the steel caught the sunlight. At first, I thought it may have evaded Morgan's notice, but a harsh chuckle escaped the sour frown he wore.

"What's wrong, fancy? Afraid of a blade?" Morgan asked.

Jeremiah laughed so hard he dropped the knife. His cheeks reddened as he bent to recover it.

"I'm not overly fond, if you must know." I made a show of eyeing Harden's revolver. "Should violence be required, I prefer to keep a respectable distance."

Morgan spat in answer. "I'll bet. Tell me, Locke, you a betting man?"

"If the mood strikes."

He glanced at Jeremiah and chuckled. "Well, hopefully you're in the mood, 'cause I'm bettin' you ain't ever seen nothin' like this." Having repeated the company line, Morgan handed Jeremiah the reins and gestured for us to follow.

"Can't make no apologies for Morgan, but don't mind the boy," Harden whispered. "Morgan's still training him. Jeremiah ain't seen nothin' like this 'til recently. Still wrapping his head around the things that men can do to one another."

I nodded. "Aren't we all?"

We tailed close behind Morgan, while Jeremiah hung back with the horses. The harsh breathing of the steam engine and the passengers' chatter softened as we walked along the tracks, leaving both behind.

Maybe fifty feet in front of the halted train lay a brutalized corpse. Blood and barbarity made the human beneath unrecognizable. Though I retained a stoic expression, I must admit this was one of the more ravaged bodies I had ever laid eyes upon.

"I can't imagine they turn up like this in Boston," Harden said, his voice soft and reverent. His trailing eyes seemed more interested in me than the corpse at our feet.

"You are not wrong, Mr. Harden." I crouched for a closer inspection. Dark crimson streaks that bordered on black obscured the identity of the victim and, to the untrained eye, hid the method of their execution.

"Burned, you think?" A curious tone had overtaken Harden's voice. Perhaps a test.

"I think not. Dark and unpleasant as the body may appear, smell the air. Have any of you gentlemen ever come in contact with a burned corpse before?"

Morgan and Harden nodded in unison.

"Then you will know it is not an aroma one forgets. And it tends to change one's dietary habits."

"So, then what do you make of it?" asked Harden, stroking his chin.

"Hmm, I regret to inform you that this unfortunate person has been flayed."

Two blank stares.

"Skinned. Most likely while still alive. I should also add that they have been here for some time, cooking in the midday sun, as it were."

"Mr. Locke," said Harden, glancing sidelong at Morgan. "Who the fuck are you?"

I grinned and opened my mouth to reply when a shout cut me off.

"Goddammit, Harden! You gonna keep us in this sweatbox all day?"

Despite my recent arrival, the boisterous voice rang familiar. Fowler, the bear of a man, once more hung out the train window to make his grievances known. Jeremiah chuckled from his position beside the engine, but Harden ignored the shouts. Morgan rolled his eyes.

"I see you there, Morgan," shouted the brash voice again. "Don't you need to be gettin' on your way? Find a hooker to suck that pitiful excuse for a pecker?"

"Fuck's sake," growled Morgan, his face taking on the shade of a ripe tomato. He stomped toward the train. "Jeremiah, give me the goddamn knife."

Jeremiah's eyes went wide, but Harden cut the tension with a laugh. "Let it go, Virgil. Don't do anything stupid. Big bastard thinks he's a cowboy. Don't give his shitty little fire any air. Real cowboys don't even wear those red sashes. That's just a story what floated down from Wyoming."

Morgan shook his head. "Got a point, John," he muttered. Although he did not ask for the knife again, Morgan's cheeks retained their furious red hue.

"Gentlemen," I interrupted. "Not to lend too much credence to Mr. Fowler's rumblings, but perhaps it would be best to move the body."

Three nods, and the unconditional acceptance of my services.

Buzzard's Edge's finest dragged the body from the tracks, leaving a rusty red trail of blood behind to paint the sand. After sharing an obscene gesture, Mr. Fowler took his seat and ceased his complaints as the train rumbled off into the distance, prepared to cover the final five-minute stretch to the center of town.

Harden slung the body over the back of his horse and invited me to walk by his side as he led the way back to town. Morgan and Jeremiah mounted their steeds and though neither man protested my inclusion, they traded more than a few side-eyed glances as they found a slow and steady pace behind us.

"Where are we taking the deceased?" I asked, if only to break the silence.

"Mr. Meyer's place," said Harden. "Purveyor of all things cobbled and wooden, and the Buzzard's Edge undertaker to boot."

There seemed nothing else to say, so I let the crunch of sand and the whisper of the warm breeze fill the air as we walked.

Upon our arrival, Mr. Meyer wordlessly directed the four of us to his workspace. He cleared a heap of tools off a table in the center of the room and helped us lay the body down, arms and legs splayed, but with fists closed tight. With only a nod of his head, he left us to gather around the table like cardinal directions on a compass.

"Jesus Christ," whispered Jeremiah. He stepped back as his pallor took on a green hue.

Harden leaned over to him. "You can wait outside. If you want." A comforting gesture, but Jeremiah remained frozen in place, eyes locked on the ghastly cadaver occupying the table.

I cleared my throat. "Sheriff, you showed little surprise when I first posited the theory of a skinned man, and if you will excuse my saying so, your question of a burn victim lacked conviction." I kept my gaze on the corpse, a man of indeterminate age.

"We suspected as much. The skinning, that is. Haven't been exactly straight with you, Mr. Locke. Wanted to see what you were made of." Harden took a breath, then loudly exhaled. "This here's the third such victim to turn up this week missing their outermost layer to shield 'em from the elements."

"All of 'em was left outside of town in the type of unidentifiable state you see here," added Morgan. "Harden might not have showed no surprise, but an outsider who turns up and nails down that method of killin' within a few seconds sure as hell catches my attention."

I turned to meet Morgan's hard stare. He had tiptoed to the line of accusation, but he would go no further—not without some kind of proof.

Harden stepped between us. "Cut the shit, Virgil. Thaddeus here was on the fuckin' train when it happened."

"And where exactly were you comin' from?" he snapped.

"Tucson," I replied, "and Tuscaloosa before that, should you need further alibi from a man attempting to help you solve this murder." I took a deep breath as I watched the arrogance drain from Morgan's face.

Harden gave a barely perceptible nod and continued. "Morgan's right—'bout the deaths, that is."

"So, what can you tell us?" asked Morgan. He nearly succeeded in keeping the edge from his voice, but a trace cut through, nonetheless.

I leaned in, squinting. "This hardly narrows the suspect pool, but this act was not performed by a medical professional." I gestured at a spot at the base of the victim's neck. "The edges are far too frayed. Even with a dull implement, a person with some knowledge of human anatomy would know how to separate skin from muscle without so much … sawing. Tearing."

Harden said nothing, but his eyes held a trace of discomfort.

Jeremiah broke from his stupor and stepped out of the room.

Any coloring the Arizona sun had imbued upon Morgan vanished. "What would you say they used?"

"Given the ragged ribbons of flesh, a knife, but something small. More appropriate for paring fingernails than separating flesh from muscle."

"Don't suppose you see anything else that could tell us who or what to look for?" asked Harden, still muffled behind his hand.

I stood to my full height and met each man's eyes before speaking. "Some of this is mere speculation, but …"

"Don't be shy, Locke," said Morgan.

"The clotting suggests the task began when the victim was alive but concluded after they had expired. As I mentioned, the ragged remains of the flesh speak to the force of the removal. You're looking for a man or woman with great strength. And with a cruel, vindictive streak to boot. Only a madman could inflict this level of suffering upon a person without personal vengeance in mind. If we can discover a motive for revenge, you'll likely have your killer in tow."

"Shit's sake … Only one glaring problem with that," said Morgan. "We don't even know who this is."

Silence shrouded the air as I studied the victim, my eyes finally landing on his closed fist. "I wonder …"

Before either Harden or Morgan could stop me, I grasped the fist and wrestled the fingers open. They remained stiff and fought me through and through, but finally gave way with a terrible crack. A smile crossed my face as I held the small metal disc up to the light. The windows allowed only a pittance of sunshine through, but it was enough to read by.

"What the hell is that?" asked Morgan.

"A soldier's medallion, and perhaps the identity of the deceased." Squinting, I scraped a patch of dried blood off the face of the medallion. "Are either of you gentlemen familiar with a former Union soldier named Joseph Flanagan?"

Harden and Morgan stared at me, jaws slack and disbelief in their eyes.

When our trio had gleaned all possible knowledge from the body, we located Jeremiah and convened at the sheriff's quarters. An uncomfortable silence hung in the air as four internal debates took place.

Morgan spoke first, shaking his head. "I need to go wash up before we do anything else. Feels like I got a dead man stink livin' in my clothes. Won't be able to focus 'til I get rid of it."

Harden nodded absently, and Morgan slipped out the door into the afternoon sun.

After a few moments, Harden spoke. "Assuming that body does belong to Joseph Flanagan, he had a wife—widow now, I suppose. A child, too. Couldn't be older than ten, if memory serves. Jeremiah, you'll come help me see if Joseph's missing. Inform the wife of what we found if need be. Mr. Locke, you're welcome to tag along."

"I'm not sure my presence would be appropriate," I said. "I believe I'll wait here."

Harden nodded. "Soon as you said that name …" He let his eyes trail to the dusty floorboards. "We know Joseph Flanagan well 'round here. Just didn't recognize him in that state."

I narrowed my eyes. "In what capacity do you know him?"

"He didn't care much for the law, I'm afraid. Nor the men who uphold it, like you and me." Harden's eyes went wide. "Not a killer, nothin' like that. Mostly minor offenses that got him locked up for a day or two. Some theft, a little robbery, always unarmed. All in all, a string of petty shit longer'n my johnson."

"Johnson?"

Harden turned red. "Never mind. Just thinkin' he must've got himself caught up in something. More I think about it, the more I expect that's him in Meyer's backroom. Anyway, I'll see what I can get out of his widow, sweet little lady by the name of Samantha."

I put my hand on his shoulder as he turned to leave. "Any name will do as a place to start. Be merciful, John, but relentless."

"You think?"

"It has always served me well."

Harden nodded, his face impassive. His countenance was that of a man who knew his duty. Western law men had earned a reputation in the east for being vicious, if not all that bright. Mr. Harden brought a solemn thoughtfulness to his work, making him a worthy adversary to anyone cold-blooded enough to stand against him.

John Harden and Jeremiah picked up their hats and walked outside. I made myself scarce in the dusty and unkempt station.

Harden burst through the office door just over an hour later. Jeremiah followed close behind.

"Shit in a bucket … I was right," said the sheriff in a sullen tone.

"Do tell, John," I replied.

Jeremiah leaned against the wall and pursed his lips. "Damn, friend. You're sweatier'n a jalapeño's armpit. Feelin' alright?"

A peal of laughter escaped my lips. "Quite. Though the Arizona sun will take some getting used to. John was correct in his earlier assessment; I may need some clothes in a shade other than black."

"Got that right." Jeremiah laughed and settled back. "Tell him, Sheriff."

Harden nodded. "No sign of Flanagan. Samantha hadn't seen him since yesterday morning. She's a lovely woman, like I said, but she didn't give two good goddamns about how her late husband made money, so long as he made it."

"Truth told, once we told her what we suspected, money seemed the only part she was broken up about," added Jeremiah.

"Interesting," I said, steepling my fingers on top of Harden's desk. "Am I to take it she was privy to Mr. Flanagan's illegal activities?"

He slammed his hat down in front of me and scratched at his balding head. "Certainly seems like he didn't hide no details from her. And now that he's dead, she didn't see no reason to protect him."

"A bold notion," I reasoned. "Has she grounds to fear legal consequences for knowledge of his crimes?"

Harden looked to Jeremiah for a moment. When his gaze returned to me, something twinkled in his eye. "That's the difference between where you come from, Mr. Locke, and where you are now. We follow a code, a set of guidelines, that helps us protect the innocent. Most times that lines up with punishing the wicked, but that ain't always the case."

"So I see." Leaning back in Harden's chair, I let a moment pass. A palette cleanser to return to the more vital subject at hand. "When you said you were right …"

"Ah …" The humble embarrassment dropped from Harden's face, and he replaced his hat upon his head. "That. Yeah, so like I said, Samantha knew the ins and outs of Flanagan's business. She said he always worked alone, that he knew he could make a little more scratch taking on bigger operations with a partner, but that he didn't trust nobody."

"Now, we're getting somewhere. Excellent work, Mr. Harden. And why should Mr. Flanagan be so bereft of trust?"

"Don't rightly know. She said he'd always been that way, since long before she met him."

"And how long ago was that?"

"About ten years, when he first moved to town from Texas. He caught her eye, and that was that."

"Hmm, so she offered no clue as to any potential enemies the man could have on the wrong side of the law? Think, Mr. Harden. Think very hard."

Harden dropped his gaze, seeming to find his feet very interesting all of the sudden.

Jeremiah cleared his throat. "Like Mr. Harden said, Joseph Flanagan was no friend of the sheriff's office. His wife seemed to think there was one law man in particular who had it out for him."

Harden raised his head and shot Jeremiah a cold stare. The young man withered under his gaze.

I sat straight up. "Yes?"

Harden had opened his mouth to answer, when the door burst open once more.

Morgan filled the doorway. "Come quick, John. There's been another murder."

Harden flew from the room, and without waiting for an invitation, I followed.

I did not need to approach the body to know this was the work of the same killer. Tossed unceremoniously in an alley behind Lynch's Tavern, this corpse sang the same tune as the last. All of the skin had been peeled from the bear-sized body, leaving the person an unrecognizable mass of bloodstained chaos.

"Once again, the ragged edges speak of pain and inexperience on the part of the butcher." As I bent down, I removed a handkerchief from my breast pocket and held it in front of my mouth and nose. Though the cadaver on the tracks reeked of hours spent decaying under the blazing Arizona sun, the freshness of this body troubled my compatriots into silence.

Jeremiah turned that familiar shade of green.

"Go get Meyer," said Harden. "Tell him we could use some more help." He watched Jeremiah turn tail and run. "Kid ain't got no stomach for this," he added as an aside to Morgan.

"They was days apart before. Now, two in a few hours. Shit, boss. This ain't good," said Morgan, his eyes darting from side to side. He removed his hat and wiped the sweat from his brow.

"No, Virgil, it surely ain't." Harden's eyes appeared sad, fixed on a detail he did not see fit to talk about yet.

Much of detective work requires instinct and the ability to make an improvised split-second decision. In that moment, I knew what Harden was about to share with me in his office and why he had truly sent Jeremiah away.

"Mr. Morgan," I whispered. "There is blood upon your shirt."

Morgan's eyebrows furrowed. "Well, shit. Yeah, of course there is." He gestured to the skinned cadaver. "Must've got some on me when I stumbled across the victim." The pace of his breathing increased as he stared back and forth between John and I. His glistening eyes betrayed realization of the off-hand comment as an accusation. "John?" he pleaded.

Harden kept his eyes on the desecrated remains. "That little red sash right there?" He pointed to a patch of scarlet fabric half-tucked under the body. Only a trained eye could have distinguished the small piece of clothing from the gore surrounding it. "That guy on the train you had it out with earlier … Fowler. He wore one just like it. Add that to the size of this here body and I think we got ourselves an identification."

Morgan's eyes ignited. "What the fuck are you trying to say, John?"

Harden shook his head. "Ain't sayin' nothin' just yet. Think we need to get this fella cleaned up and off the street. Then we need to have ourselves a conversation." His next words were careful and measured. "Will you help us, Virgil?"

Morgan took a step back. He licked his lips and stared daggers at me. "What kind of poisonous bullshit has this carpetbagger put in your head, John?"

With a sigh, Harden answered. "Not a lick that wasn't already brewin' in there, I'm afraid. I'll ask again, Virgil. Will you help us and come along? If you don't want to answer this time, the question's gonna change."

"Fuck you," spat Morgan.

"Shit," whispered Harden—heartbreak resonated in the single word. A friend and a brother-in-arms turned killer. He reached for his revolver, but Morgan punched him square in the eye. Harden crashed to the ground in a plume of dust as Morgan turned and bolted from the alley.

Snatching Harden's firearm, I gave chase.

I burst from the alley to see a blur of a human being disappear behind the tavern. My late-night detective work usually called for more exercise of the mind than the body, but I took pains to remain in shape for such an occasion as this. Rounding the corner dropped me onto a straight narrow road, Morgan at least one hundred paces ahead of me.

The citizens crowding the streets either took no notice or cared not a whit about the two men barreling through. I barked out repeated "excuse mes" and "pardons," slamming into men and women both in an attempt to close the gap between Morgan and myself. Near the end of the road, he glanced over his shoulder, then ducked between two buildings—another alley. With exhaustion setting in, I pushed myself to run harder, faster. If he vanished in that alcove, all was lost with him.

I skidded to a stop just before the opening, a small crevice between a barber shop and a telegraph office. Taking in a deep breath in case it was my last, I darted around the corner. I anticipated two possibilities—either no sign of my quarry or a loaded pistol aimed between my eyes. Yet I came upon neither. Instead, Virgil Morgan sat collapsed in a heap, pitched against a wall in the abandoned alley. Tears cut trails through the grime caked on his face.

When he caught sight of me, he furiously wiped them away. "Son of a bitch," he whimpered. "Why did I run, Mr. Locke?"

I leveled the sheriff's revolver at Morgan's head and glanced around. Not a soul in sight. "Whatever do you mean, Virgil?"

"I ain't never killed nobody that didn't have it coming. Not outside the confines of the law, anyway. Got me a temper, but hell, John's always known that. How could he think I'd be capable of … of doin' that to a person?"

The flicker of a grin settled on my face, though I kept the revolver aimed at Morgan. "Because all the evidence points to you. Fowler's sash, your multiple run-ins with Joseph Flanagan. Even the first two victims tie to your name."

Morgan squinted. When he spoke, his voice trembled in a mixture of fear and confusion. "How could you know that?"

"I made sure of it." I glanced around again, but we remained very much alone. "You see, Mr. Morgan, I have a propensity for distributing death. With such an inclination, it is never wise to stay in one area for very long. Even for that short period of time, one must ingratiate themselves within the community. It has worked for me in various small towns in and around New England, most recently in Cambridge. You see, a teacher arrives in town with a degree of dignity. Respect, if you like. Yet, they remain an outsider, and outsiders are always the first suspects when things go wrong."

Morgan grinded his teeth together, yet he offered not a word. The fury in his eyes from earlier paled in comparison to the blaze that filled them now.

"Bodies are found under mysterious circumstances and, of course, the town will search for someone to blame. The less familiar, the better. But what if that new arrival helped to solve the crime? Furthermore, what if that person could unmask the murderer as a respected member of the community? A priest, a town councilman, a—"

"Sheriff's deputy?" Though hate filled Morgan's eyes, a smirk crept across his face.

I nodded in acquiescence.

"And when you've caught me and the killings don't stop?"

"Oh, they will stop. For a time, at least. Until the itch becomes too much again. Then, I will gracefully bow out and relocate. Mr. Morgan, I think you'd be surprised at my self-discipline. I can hold out for quite some time."

"John'll find you out. He ain't stupid."

"No. No, he is not, but you asked me earlier if I was a betting man? Thus far, Mr. Harden does not realize I have been squatting in town for a week already, listening and learning, moving about only under cover of darkness. He does not suspect that I boarded the train only a few miles outside of town as a stowaway, or that I changed from my clothes, soaked in Fowler's blood, while he was interviewing Samantha Flanagan. Shall I go on?"

"You ain't actually scared of knives, are ya?"

With a chuckle, I continued. "If I were a betting man, I'd bet on Mr. Harden being more like those eastern sheriffs than he fancies himself and only seeing what he wants to see."

"Well, then," said Morgan. "Seems you've thought of everything."

"In fact, I pride myself on it."

"Then you already know you can't let me live. I'll sing like a canary."

I cocked my head to the side. "My scapegoats never do make it out alive. Though, I will say, this is the first time I've had to pull the trigger myself."

With his life in imminent danger, Morgan made no move to fight. He inhaled deeply as anger gave way to wonder in his eyes. "Now, how the hell have you managed that?"

"A trade secret for another day, I'm afraid." I smiled as I squeezed the trigger.

The calamitous gunfire drew a crowd so quickly I barely had time to fill Morgan's hand with his own gun and slip the knife I'd used on Fowler into his pocket. Harden, a black-and-purple bruise already forming around his eye, pushed through the crowd. His jaw dropped and his features sank as he took in the grizzled sight of his former deputy. Ribbons of gore entwined with bits of skull littered the alleyway, all that remained of the murderous mind of Virgil Morgan.

I forced tears to the corner of my eyes and laid a hand upon Harden's shoulder. "I am deeply sorry, John. He left me no choice."

Harden nodded but said nothing. He studied Morgan's body for a moment or two, then turned his back on it. "Christ almighty, Mr. Locke. Thad. It all right if I call you Thad?"

"Of course."

"I just never thought he had it in him. I trusted Virgil with my life and … shit. To think he was capable of that. Makes my skin crawl, you know?"

"I do not wish to seem indelicate, but who will take care of Mr. Morgan and Mr. Fowler?"

"Anyone but me, for the moment. I need some time to get my head straight before I talk to Jeremiah. Be a wonder if the kid sticks around after this." He sighed, then met my eyes. "I wouldn't hate the company, though. Would you walk with me?"

"I should be honored."

We exited the alleyway and walked slowly down the main stretch of town that led to the sheriff's office.

"You never did tell me what brought you to Buzzard's Edge," said Harden.

"New opportunities, John. Though it seems of such little import right now. I hope you will not think me perverse, but despite today's events, I quite like it here. A nice change of pace from the hustle and bustle of life back east. Do you happen to know if Buzzard's Edge has need of an educator?"

"I can point you toward someone who'd know, and I wouldn't mind having those investigative skills to call on every so often." Harden raised his eyebrows as though he'd asked a question.

"Certainly. I am ever at your disposal."

A grin wiped the dour expression from John Harden's face. He clapped a hand on my back as we walked away from the carnage and commotion.

THE REAPING, PART VI

Blood drains from Josiah's face, even as his cheeks blaze. Words flutter in his head, refusing to follow a straight and narrow path to his lips.

Vulture plops to the sand, stares at Josiah as though his expression has become worrying.

My, those talons are sharp, he thinks.

"What do you mean the railroad tracks haven't been built yet?" Josiah chokes out the words.

"Past, present, and what is to come," says Vulture, taking on the solemn tone of a priest warning about the dangers of a fiery afterlife. "I told you these stories traverse all three."

"But … but how? W-witchcraft. Surely, witchcraft." His knees wobble, threatening to spill him to the sand. Only the cunning glint in Coyote's eye sturdies his gait.

"Calm down, Josiah," says Coyote. "Bound to give yourself a fit."

"Witchcraft." Vulture says the word as though he can taste each syllable. "You're free to use the word, of course, though I don't believe it's the right one." The bird's milky eye studies him from head to toe, as if assessing the possibility of danger. "In a way, this sight comes as naturally as rocks break down to sand over centuries. Time and pressure imposing their will on us all. A burden, Mr. Dennis, to know what's aimed directly at you, and be unable to change the course of events, but an all-seeing eye comes with benefits."

"Such as?" Coyote asks in a practiced manner that sends a chill up Josiah's spine.

"When someone tells a story that rings with half-truth, it's quite easy to parse out the falsehoods."

Josiah's stomach twists. "What are you saying, you mangy fuckin' bird?"

Vulture slides forward, talons scratching at the sand. A shadow passes over its face, though there are no birds in the sky to cast it.

"Plainly, that you have not shared your entire story. There are Apache in the region, that much is true, and some of them are violent, yes. Why, they even bleed the same hue as that on your hatchet. Clearly, you've thought through the tale at great length."

Coyote lets out a low whimper. "The shop that will belong to Nola is straight head, Vulture. Want me to take this one?"

Vulture sits still as a statue for a moment, two, then nods toward Coyote without tearing its eyes from Josiah.

"You murdered those people, Josiah. The why is beyond me, but I see the how and the when. I can even see that your party was not four, but five. Yourself, of course. Your wife, Annabelle. The other couple, Ezekiel and Esther. But there was another." It shakes its head, slowly. "A child. What carries a man to that point?"

Coyote turns away. It doesn't see Josiah blanch to the hue of a ghost, the word "Elizabeth" dancing across his lips.

SALVIA SUNSET

My name is Leanora Betts, but this town calls me Nola. Don't exactly remember how it started, maybe as simple as somebody mixing up the letters in my first name. Buzzard's Edge isn't known for being home to the best and brightest. Either way, it stuck. So hard, in fact, that when the time came to make a sign for the tailor shop my daddy left me, and Mr. Meyer asked what I wanted etched into the wood, I only hesitated a second before answering with a grin.

Nola's.

Enough about that, though. I suppose I started writing this here diary to tell you about a monster. Now y'all got me halfway between spinning a yarn and trying to drum up some business.

When the sun starts to shake hands with the tops of the buildings on the western edge of town, that's when I usually close up shop. That first night, I opened the door to the deserted street, flipped the sign to "closed," and winked at the setting sun as it threw heavenly shades of purple across the sand. With calloused fingers, immune to the heat of matches and the poke of needles, I slid the bolt that keeps late arrivals out of the store and started toward the backroom to prepare a light supper. Then my feet froze in place before my mind could even catch up.

What did I see? I thought.

Purple sand. No, red sand.

Blood?

My heart raced like a jackrabbit as I eased back to the door, resting one hand on the bolt. The other searched out the derringer I always keep on my person. It's not often I get a customer arguing about prices, and it's never the same person twice. Besides, a woman who works alone can never be too careful.

The *click* of the door bolt sounded like a dropped rifle hammer as I slid it open, and the door squealed on its hinges, announcing my presence to the—I hoped—empty street. In the thirty seconds since my last gaze out at the street, the sun had fallen miles and taken the beautiful desert salvia purple hue with it. At the mouth of the alley that meets the store's steps, a dark liquid puddled under the fading light.

One thing you learn about Buzzard's Edge. Talk to most people and they'll tell you the sand here drinks blood fast as a shot of whiskey. Except the sand didn't seem to be in any kind of rush that night.

Eyes wide for any sign of movement, I squeezed the derringer's grip until my knuckles popped.

A shift in the shadows and a low growl drifted out from the alleyway, a deep rumble like two boulders grinding together in the blazing darkness. Between threatening snarls, I heard the wet crunch of bone marrying the squish of teeth biting through tender meat.

An animal.

Moonlight glinted off two midnight-black orbs in the shadows, large enough to fill a fist and staring straight at me from only a foot or two off the ground. Razor-thin pupils surrounded by flecks of fiery orange embers. The chewing stopped, replaced by a thin hiss, then the creature's body whooshed against the sand as it approached, the sound of an exhale so big it could've come from God himself.

A big fucking animal.

My gut clenched, and I stumbled back inside, fingers feeling for the door, and unable to take my eyes off the monster.

The demon eyes drew closer, only a little, but an outline formed around them. Head wider than a wagon wheel and flat on top, with orange fire dancing along the edge of its skull.

Finally, I laid hands on the splinter-riddled wood of the door. Muscle memory kicked in and in one swift motion, I threw the door shut and drove home the bolt.

Then I waited, staring down that little slab of metal, praying it just might prove enough to keep such a monstrosity at bay. Time crawled, I swear. Every creaking board, flutter of wind made me sure I'd be that beast's next meal. But minute after minute passed, and the door stood firm, keeping out the wider world.

Sprawled across the floor and surrounded by drapes of fabric, I closed my eyes. Even in that self-imposed darkness, I could see the jagged shadow behind those inhuman eyes. Unnatural and misshapen.

What kind of animal roaming the Arizona desert looked like that?

The question danced around the edges of my mind, pushing away any remaining thoughts of supper.

I ain't proud to admit it, but I spent most of the night curled up on the floorboards, eyes locked on that door, waiting for the inevitable. Or maybe wondering if I imagined the whole thing.

I was still there, exhausted, when the sun started peeking around the edges of the tarp-covered windows.

"Christ a'mighty, Miss Nola. You look like ten shades of hell."

Leaning on one hand against the counter, I forced a smile. "Thanks for the kind words, Pete. And just as much for the dirt you tracked in behind you."

"Can't be helped," said Pete, with a look that said it probably could've been helped. He set his pickaxe on the counter and let that guilty grin slip into something a little more charming. Or at least what passed for charming in his mind.

You wish, I thought, but straightened up anyway. Let a man in your bed once and he'll live in your head forever. "Long night with some less than perfect sleep." I bit my tongue, hoping he missed the opening I just gave him. "What can I help you with?"

Pete thumped a pair of worn moleskin pants on the counter and stepped back as a puff of dust erupted out of them. How a single person could house so much grime is beyond me.

"Patch them up?" I asked.

"If you'd be so kind." Pete cracked his neck, then looked down at his outfit. "Lucky for me, I got extras. It's dark underground and everything seems to have a sharp edge. Even the mighty work of Nola Betts ain't no match for what they got down there."

I tilted an eyebrow up. "And what do they got down there?"

Pete turned, checking to make sure the store was still deserted, except for the two of us. Still, he leaned forward and kept his voice down. "Really wanna know?"

As much as I hate to admit it, I was curious. I flashed a quick nod and watched Pete lick his lips, like the secret he was about to unveil just might change the fabric of Buzzard's Edge, make everybody under that harsh Arizona sun filthy rich.

"Jack shit." He slammed a fist on the counter, and I nearly jumped. "The occasional Gila monster out there away from the population, but I have a hard time believing those fat little sausages are as dangerous as people make out."

"Poison breath, my daddy always said." I shrugged. "Kill you with a single bite."

"Didn't say I got close enough to find out. Creepy things, though." The smile that had been climbing the side of Pete Navarro's face the last few minutes dropped as he shook his head. "Boss told us we'd find a vein of gold running like blood through a healthy man. Don't nothin' down there shine except the flickering lantern lights. Thirteen weeks of blood, sweat, and stone, we ain't got nothin' to show for it."

He held a finger to his lips and let his eyes fill in the blanks.

Message received, loud and clear. *But you didn't hear it from me.*

I leaned over the counter, looking down and pretending to inspect what Pete'd brought me. "Suppose the boss doesn't want the wives to know he's taking their husbands away for naught."

Pete winked. "And with no guarantee of a proper payday, neither. Not that Mr. Farrell cares about that."

"One of the benefits of being my own boss." I winked back and pushed the dusty pants aside. Torn seam. Fifteen, maybe twenty minutes' worth of work. If what he said about the dry mining gig was true, maybe I could knock a little off the price tag. Just this once.

"So why do you keep going down?" I asked.

"Seriously?"

"Of course."

Pete Navarro stroked the stubble along his chin, just for show. He knew the answer before I asked the question. I'm sure of it.

"Hope," he said, after a beat. "Man with the amount of power Farrell has starts digging a hole, you can be sure he checked his math first. Just yesterday, we opened up a new chamber. Be just my luck I'd throw down my pickaxe and the rest of the guys'd find nugget heaven in that unexplored cavern."

I sucked at my teeth, weighing my next words with care. "I don't doubt Mr. Farrell checked his math, but sometimes a man like him is just too damn stubborn to admit he was wrong. Man like that has the money to just keep you all digging 'til you come out the other side of the earth. Or maybe you find something you weren't meant to find."

Truth be told, I thought about the alley just then. The same one I'd been too cowardly to explore when I'd opened the shop that morning.

Pete narrowed his eyes. "What's that mean?"

"Nothing." A shudder ran across my shoulders, and I could tell he saw it. "You seen anything … unusual around here lately? I don't know, heard about anybody going missing?"

The words sounded crazy as they left my mouth. Not for the first time, I wondered what, if anything, I'd really seen the night before.

Beneath his coal black stubble, Pete went toad-belly white. "Why? What you heard?"

He sounded angry. I backed up a step or two before remembering the cold metal at my back. I could pull the gun before Pete hopped the counter if it came to that. "Just a strange night is all." I let out a sigh, and he deflated a bit like the wind had come from him. "Bad dreams, Pete."

He dropped his shoulders, eased his posture. Not quite comfortable, but less predatory. His eyes glazed a bit. "Matter of fact," he said, "Man went missing last night." Pete warded off an unasked question with a shake of his head. "Not in the mines, though there's enough twists and turns down there to make it a real possibility. Naw, Tim Langan. You know him?"

"Little bit." An understatement. I knew all the miners. Never met a crew so hard on their clothes.

"What I expected. His lady, Julia, she stops me this morning. Not half an hour ago on my way here. Says Tim never came home last night."

"So how do you know he came up from the mine?" My voice sounded distant, like it belonged to a stranger. I thought of purple skies, crimson puddles, teeth scraping bone.

"Had a drink with him after we called it a day. Just one," he said in a defensive tone. "Just one. Then Tim stumbled out of Lynch's Tavern and set out on his way. Never saw him again. Now I hear he's missing. Guess I got a little upset, is all." He lowered his eyes like he didn't trust what might show in them.

My hand shot across the counter before I could stop it and took his. What I expected to see come across his face, I don't know, but what I got was surprise with a side of pity. I let my eyes flick down to the pants dirtying up the counter. "I'll have these ready to go by the time Farrell lets you off." I bit my lip and held his gaze. "Promise you'll be careful."

"Yeah," he choked out. "Of course."

My hand lingered on his a moment longer, then I slowly drew it back, picking up a stray needle just for something else to hold.

Pete Navarro backed toward the door, some kind of wounded animal look drawn on his face, and tipped his hat as he ducked outside. Something shone in his eyes as he left. Fear wouldn't be the wrong word to put on it, but with a touch of softness.

After brushing a desert's worth of dust off the moleskin pants he'd left, I stitched them up quick and perfect. Less than fifteen minutes. A swift fold then up and over the wooden rack behind the counter, one task done before the day even truly commenced. Customers, both regular and prospective, flowed in and out of the store like a piddling creek throughout the day. Steady enough, but hardly an undammed river. I smiled, laughed, made pleasant conversation, but never quite shook the nerves Pete left me with.

Never quite shook the creature's eyes from the night before, neither.

The sun ambled across the sky and that lovely purple light started to paint the floorboards once more. Pete's work pants hung like an executed prisoner, waiting for God to ferry them away.

Only Pete never showed up to claim them.

That night, I bolted the door without opening it first. As far as I know, the sign read 'open' all night long.

When the rooster living out behind Barron's Apothecary crowed, I stayed in bed. When the children passed by, hooting and hollering on their way to the schoolhouse, I stayed in bed.

An occasional knock came from out front, always following a curious jiggle at the door handle and the bolt rocking in its place. Not Pete. I like to think I'd have known his knock. A moment later, tentative footsteps traveled in the opposite direction, likely under the assumption Miss Nola had run off to see to an errand.

The darkest thoughts cycled through my mind. Black, beady eyes, a slobbering mouth, crunching bones. Pete's countenance, eyes wide with fear instead of smugly narrow.

Confident. It's a better word.

After careful consideration, I decided against opening the shop. All the work orders were closed out and I could stand to lose a day's income without resorting to eating sand. I rolled out of bed and dressed, topping the outfit off with a dark gray Stetson, which did a passable job of holding up my raven-colored hair. An unplanned day off, but I'd use it to its fullest advantage. Couldn't avoid staring down that alley forever, so while the Arizona sun lorded over the people of Buzzard's Edge and the monstrous eyes had no shadows to hide among, I'd pick up some thread.

And if I happened to run into some people I could bat my eyes at and pepper with a few questions about just what the fuck was going on, all the better. Maybe I'd even stop by Pete's house.

As I stepped out the front door for the first time in two days, the quiet overwhelmed me. Mr. Locke keeping the students silent with an iron fist, no doubt, but there were less people wandering the streets than usual for the time of day. The vacant alleyway wouldn't let me pass without a careful inspection and that's alright, because under the mid-morning sun, there was no place to hide in there. Scratches in the sand, blood and bones. Gristle. I expected every bit but found nothing.

There's that old adage again. Buzzard's Edge sand drinks blood, but the lack of a crime scene made my head spin. Did I imagine it after all?

If memory served, I'd heard Pete talk about living on the outskirts, so that's where I headed. Spent most of the walk mumbling under my breath about finding him laid up in bed, sick from a harmless little cold or maybe just tired of going to work. The last made me laugh out loud and drew odd looks from the few people walking the streets.

Past the tavern, past the barbershop, the businesses gave way to homes. I'd never been to Pete's place, so I didn't quite know what to look for, and I never did find out.

"Teeth bigger'n my hand and a tail, I tells ya."

Charlie Brooks stood with his back to the desert like he was preaching a homily to the worn wooden buildings at the edge of town.

My stomach flipped. Another miner stood before him, decked out in tan pants and flannel shirts, too damn hot for Buzzard's Edge in the summer, but protection trumps comfort when you spend most of your daylight hours under the ground.

You're full of shit, Charlie.

I waited for the other man to say so, but he held his tongue. Charlie filled the silence again, teetering as he spoke. To be honest, my heart sank a little because it sure sounded like Crooked Charlie was talking about my night beast and even at a little after nine in the morning his words blended together like a crosshatch pattern.

"Telling you," he said. "Whatever it was, t'ain't down there no more, and I'll be good and goddamned before you get me back in that hole."

"Rush of wind," said the other man. I squinted and leaned forward to get a better look at his face. Chester Mills, reliable as any of the underground boys and always good for a couple extra cents on top of the agreed-upon price.

"Rush of wind'll put the lanterns out, sure, but I ain't never known no wind to up and growl as it passes." Charlie produced a flask from thin air and took a swig. "Everyone's thinking it, I'm just saying it. We dug too deep, pissed somethin' off. Somethin' big."

Mills twisted up his eyebrows. "What if we let it out, Charlie? Think about it. First Langan, then Paulson and Stephens all in one go. Now I hear ... Christ."

The words hung in the air, even keeping Charlie's tongue from flapping.

That's when I realized I'd been spotted. I let out a long-held breath.

"Miss Nola," Mills called out with a little leftover shake in his voice. He tried to let something pleasant settle over his face, but his eyebrows remained in a fit of consternation.

"Looking for Pete," I said, suddenly sure that was the name about to escape Chester's lips. "Pete Navarro. Never picked up his order yesterday."

The two men traded a look that said my thinking was dead on. My throat tightened, and I held my breath again.

Charlie lost the staredown and took off his hat, letting the sun beat down on his leathery head. "Don't rightly know where he is, Miss Nola. Never showed up this morning." He glanced toward Mills and received a quick nod in return. "Pete and two others. Couldn't nobody tell Mr. Farrell where they got off to, and hoo boy, I ain't never seen the boss so dang mad. Face turned redder'n a brushfire, and he started shouting—"

"Some things you ought not repeat in front of a lady," Mills chimed in.

I waved away the attempt at chivalry. "What's being done?"

"Well," said Charlie, looking almost tight-lipped for the first time in his life. "Mr. Farrell stormed off to look into some things. Told everybody to meet outside town tomorrow morning. Right around sunup."

As if on cue, a dusty group of tan-clad men ambled by, pickaxes slung over their shoulders. They looked like soldiers returning from the war between the states. Walking ghosts. The way their eyes flickered around, dancing across their surroundings, spoke of a group that felt unsafe. Like something was watching, ready to pick them off one by one.

"Where?" I asked.

"Well, there's an abandoned farmhouse half burned to the—"

Mills stamped on Charlie's foot.

"I know it," I said.

"Best be going." Mills cleared his throat and nodded in the direction I'd come from. "I'd steer clear if I was you, Boss can demonstrate quite a temper when he gets worked up."

"So can I. Thanks all the same, Chester, but I'm keen on finding out what happened to my friend."

His face drooped. He looked to Charlie, but the other man had his flask tipped to oblivion. "Suit yourself, Miss Nola. Don't say I didn't warn you."

Without another word, Mills spun and marched off down the road after the other miners, Charlie stumbling in his wake.

A few buildings down, the miners filled the street soundlessly. Nervous eyes crawled across every shadow, warning that the fear in Charlie and Chester's voices wasn't limited to just them two.

All around the miners, Buzzard's Edge held its breath.

I never did pick up that thread.

It's fine. I had enough in the back to see me through the next few days. Spun the "closed" sign back to "open", made chit-chat with the first five or six people through the door, even fed the till enough to keep food on the table for another week. All with that same smile that said, *everything's fine.*

Just so long as you don't look too deep.

All through the day, I kept an eye out for anyone in moleskin and flannel, the unofficial uniform of the miners. They stayed away, though. Gone missing or in no mood to have their wares repaired to work another day.

Then the sun dropped, seemed to plummet that night, like somebody with greased fingers lost their grip on it. I braved the wild streets of Buzzard's Edge to turn the sign. With the door open to a crack, my breath misted out into the cooling night. Every shadow promised hateful eyes, dull and black. Every breeze threatened to carry an agonized shout.

In the end, there was nothing.

I closed and bolted the door. Then I pulled out the derringer, sat behind the counter, and waited for morning.

The wind blew and sometimes it sounded like screams, but a mind in that kind of worried state has been known to make things up.

Despite Charlie Brooks's loose lips and Chester Mills's protests, anybody with some spare time and passing curiosity could've found the meeting. Miners flocked through the otherwise lonesome streets, trudging from packed sand to the looser open Sonoran Desert, coming to a rest before a burned-out husk of a farmhouse.

If you believe the stories, a kid murdered his parents there and set the farm on fire before disappearing. The ghouls in charge of the town let it stand, maybe as a warning or because they thought it cursed. If you believe the stories. Regardless, it was a landmark everyone knew, away from prying eyes.

Except for mine, of course.

Still, I kept to the shaded areas, afraid my lead-shot lined dress might mark me as out of place. Nobody passed a glance my way, though. Once the men came to a stand-still, sweat dribbled down their temples. The morning sun, sure, but fear just as thick. Fear of death or maybe fear of what waited underground.

As the crowd began to rumble with impatience, Alexander Farrell slinked out from behind the ruins. Dressed in a midnight-black suit, which somehow evaded the dust swirling through the air, Farrell kept his eyes on the workers, like a man watching a rattlesnake at a distance. From the front lines, a few men stepped forward, dressed in the same miners' gear as all the others, but with a decidedly more menacing appearance.

Bodyguards.

Farrell cleared his throat and narrowed his eyes to silence the rabble. Only a moment passed before it got quiet enough you could've heard a drop of sweat hit the sand. A shadowy overhang kept the sun off me and provided a place to watch the speech where I wouldn't draw attention.

"You all know why I've called you here today." Farrell scowled and let the words hang in the air. He spat before he went on. "Three months since we first broke ground and now, I got men vanishing on me. Poof. Five just this week and shit, the week's not even half over."

Five. The hair stood on the back of my neck.

"Men that've done work for me before, they'll know you can't get a damn thing by me. Those whispers when you think you're all alone with a friend? I hear those. So, allow me to address a couple things. There is no, I repeat, no truth to the rumor that these men got lost in the mine. Mr. Marquez ..." He pointed to a short, round fella in the front row. "Mr. Marquez personally counts heads at the beginning and end of each day. The numbers have aligned for more than eighty consecutive workdays and I do expect they will continue to do so."

An arrogant smirk replaced the nasty glare.

"It's been said we're digging away for nothing. Busting our pickaxes and our backsides for something we're not likely to find. The whispers say this is what drives our missing men away, scampering off in the night to avoid the embarrassment of accusing me to my face. This is a lie. We knew going in this would be for the long haul. That's why I hired you men on for an indefinite period of time. And for those who stay the course, the reward will be great."

Murmurs of anger simmered like meat in a skillet.

"The last is maybe the most troubling." Farrell commanded respect, could boil a whole group of dirty, roughshod men down to just about nothing with a look and a few well-chosen words. Except this crowd didn't want to settle. Unrest sizzled through the air like the feeling before a thunderstorm. My forearm began to ache, and I realized I was digging my nails into it.

Through it all, Farrell remained impassive. "Some truly vicious, perhaps dangerous, notions flying around about … monsters in the tunnels. Frankly, it embarrasses me to have men under my employ that would bandy that horseshit about, never mind believe it." He took a moment and seemed to lock eyes with every man in the crowd.

"However, foolish or otherwise, it must be addressed. I'll not tolerate anyone spreading lies that make for an unsafe working environment, and make no mistake, my friends, contributing to the truancy of a fellow worker, leaves us undermanned and at bigger risk."

Temperatures rose. Most of the miners made no efforts to keep their voices down anymore.

"So." Farrell raised his voice to just below a shout, determined to press on with or without a captive audience. "A few new rules, some addendums, and the like." He raised his index finger.

Then a scream broke out, freezing Farrell in place. The way the blood drained from his face made me think he bought more of that horseshit than he let on.

I broke free of the shadows, no longer caring about being spotted, when a laugh caught my ear. At odds with the scream, it made confusion swirl through my head. The crowd parted like the Red Sea to reveal Chester Mills holding up his pickaxe, a black and orange lizard no bigger than a man's boot impaled on the end. One of those ferocious Gila monsters.

Charlie Brooks' sullen face admitted his role as the man behind the scream. The workers surrounding him pointed and laughed, though they kept their distance from the murdered critter.

"Alright, alright," shouted Farrell, finger still outstretched and ready to make a point. "Shut up, already. We're not done here."

Mills slung the dispatched beast into the charred remains of the farmhouse and the laughter gradually died away.

Farrell opened his mouth to continue, and a growl cut him off. Deep and low, like the movement of the earth itself. The merciless sound silenced the last remaining bouts of laughter. The ground rumbled, resonating with that menacing growl. Charred pieces of wood shivered in the morning air.

From underneath the ashy wreckage of the house, a beast the length of a Conestoga wagon shot out and seized Charlie Brooks by the leg. Dull metal caught glimpses of sunlight as the miners swung their pickaxes at the creature. Orange and black beads lined its armor-like skin, deflecting their attacks like flies trying to pass through a sheet of steel. The monster swung its bulbous head—the same wagon-wheel-sized head I'd seen the other night—and tore Charlie's leg clean off. To that point in my life, I'd never heard a man make a sound like Charlie did, like a soul on fire trying to escape its prison, and I hope to never hear it again. Venom dribbled from its pointed fangs, mixing with Charlie's blood on the charred sand to hiss and bubble.

Venom.

I shook my head in disbelief. The orange bands surrounding its pitch-black body. It couldn't be. Nothing grew that big, never mind a Gila monster.

A shot rang out, ricocheting off the lizard's stone-hard skin with a high-pitched whine before burying itself in the sand. The men scattered, leaving Charlie at the mercy of the monster. It swallowed his leg in a single gulp and crawled forward, hovering over his head. With something between a snarl and a roar, it blasted Charlie in the face with desert-hot breath. Even at a distance, I could feel the heat and smell the rot it unleashed. The screams stopped and Charlie let out a choking sound.

His tongue no longer looked like a tongue. The monster's breath had liquified it and now it poured down his throat, cutting off his airway. When I saw the skin sloughing off Charlie's face, I said a prayer that the lack of air might kill him quickly.

The great lizard stilled, twice as long as an ox and near the same height. It turned its head slowly to take in the scene. Most of the men ran for the town. Fools, putting others in danger. Some took off for the Blackjack Mountains, waving their arms and crying out as if to draw it away. Alexander Farrell stared the monster down from his improvised pulpit, suit so black it matched the charred wood behind him. His bodyguards scattered and Farrell gritted his teeth, but kept quiet. I had a hard time figuring whether it was obstinance or fear that kept him rooted to the spot. The beast dove for Farrell, arcing at the last minute to take out the rotund little man next to him.

Marquez, I thought. Not one of the miners but dressed in solidarity.

Fangs longer than a revolver barrel tore into Marquez's abdomen, spilling his guts across the sand. The lizard locked its dull killer's eyes on Farrell. A low grumble sounded in its throat and then it scuttled off, tackling another miner to the ground and sinking its jaws into the man's rib cage.

Seemingly let off the hook, Farrell collapsed to the ground and crawled away, hiding among the ruined timbers while the creature ripped his workers to shreds. A few brave souls remained behind, hacking away at the beast with their sharpened tools. They might as well have been trying to break rock with a spoon. A whip of that mighty tail and the men flew through the air. They crashed to the ground a dozen feet away and waited for the monster to choose which of them would die next.

Gleams of pearl-white teeth, stygian-black claws, glints of stone-dulled metal, blood so crimson it almost appeared purple, and flashes of flannel and moleskin.

Flannel and moleskin.

We opened up a new chamber, Pete had said.

And something escaped. What was the first thing it saw?

Flannel and moleskin.

Sacrifices from a boss man who never spent a day in his life under the earth and was about to get off scot-free for it, simply because he'd chosen to elevate himself over the others by his clothing.

The miners who were still able abandoned the fight and fled in whatever direction would have them, leaving trails of blood in their wake. The sand swallowed their tools as the giant lizard spun, searching for any new challenges. No less than ten men lay half-buried in the Sonoran, eviscerated but not yet feasted upon.

The beast stopped in its bloodthirsty rampage and stared me down. I wore a navy blue, knee-length dress that not even a mindless beast could mistake for work gear. The lead weights dragged at the hem, ensuring some semblance of propriety.

Lead.

I felt a brush of cold at my back. The creature did not attack, not yet, but nor did it seem to trust me. A sudden movement might draw its ire. I risked a look around as I draped my fingers by my side, wriggled them to loosen up for what was to come.

If any men had survived on this barren farmland, they'd made themselves as scarce as Mr. Farrell. The creature dug into the sand with a foot the size of a barstool, talons so sharp they could cut grains of sand in two. Its dark tongue flicked into the air, a last-ditch effort to establish friend from foe. When it sucked its tongue back in, I was left with only fiery orange embers dotting black beaded skin. The little derringer wouldn't even put a dimple in it.

A growl started low and climbed into the air. I wasn't dressed like the men who'd invaded its home, the men it silently swore revenge on, but it had clearly decided my intentions. Muscles rippled beneath its dotted skin as it prepared to pounce. With a hand trained to knock out a week's worth of sewing in an afternoon, I grabbed for the gun, seized it by the grip, and let fly a single shot all before the monster could leap.

I swear the shot moved so slow I watched it carve through the thick afternoon air, politely excusing itself before cracking the surface of the Gila monster's eye. I held the gun up, hand trembling, but ready to try for the other side if need be. The lizard seemed to have no interest in a rematch, letting out an anguished cry that filled the air and struck me square in the heart.

An animal, I thought. *A big fucking animal, but an animal.*

Leaking a muddy black ichor from its ruined eye, the monster stumbled over the pile of flesh and guts in the direction of the Blackjacks. From the gathering of bodies and the ashes of the house, half a dozen normal-sized Gila monsters followed.

I watched the thing scamper toward the horizon, in the direction of the mine, until it disappeared. Only then did I lower the gun. Everything became so quiet; I wondered if I might hear the sand drinking its fill of blood.

Only more silence.

"Mr. Farrell, you out there?"

A strange sound greeted me. Not quite a whimper, the man would never lower himself to that, but certainly not a true word, either.

"That thing killed a fair few of my friends, one of them a very good friend. You take my meaning?"

"Yes, ma'am," said a voice that sounded like a gelded version of the man himself.

"I don't give a shit if that mine has a vein of gold down there that'd make Midas himself jealous. You're gonna gather up any man still alive and willing, and blow the entrance. Today."

The ashes stirred, and I raised the gun just to remind him I still had it.

"How the hell do I know I'd be sealing it in?"

"Where else do you expect it's headed right now? Way I see it, Mr. Farrell, that abominably large critter only ever wanted to be left alone. You're just going to prevent any more blood on your hands by granting its wish."

"And if I disagree?"

I could see his eyes then. Bold, yeah, but not without fear. I looked straight into them and for just a second, I think we understood each other. A man like Farrell doesn't like to lose, but he's always got a new venture up his sleeve, ready to roll out when the first one becomes unprofitable, or worse, boring. Maybe a brothel next time. Put a bullet between his eyes and there'd be more men just like him, greedy and opportunistic, ready to rise up and take his place.

Neither of us said another word, and it was enough to assure me I'd hear a sizable explosion later that day.

Sure enough, barely an hour passed before an ungodly amount of dynamite made the whole of Buzzard's Edge jump. All except me. I'd waited for it, passing the time scribbling all this down. I let a little smile cross my face when it was done. Plenty of time for Big Mama, or so I'd started to think of her to tuck in, safe and dark in the heart of the earth. It wouldn't bring Pete or the others back, but it wasn't nothing either.

With the sign turned to "closed", I took Pete's moleskin pants off the rack and tucked them under the counter. I'd figure out what to do with them another day. I set up camp on the harsh wooden floor, maybe just one more night of that, and left the tarp peeled back. The monsters on the other side of the wall no longer scared me as much as they used to. Besides, the sun was turning the sky the loveliest shade of desert salvia purple.

I woke twenty minutes ago in a cold sweat, but it wasn't the harsh floor that stole my sleep. It was a vision of Big Mama, bursting out from under that pile of rubble to lay waste to Farrell's gathering. Maybe she was hiding from the sun, maybe she wasn't. Maybe the entrance to the mine that Farrell blew to holy hell earlier wasn't the only way in. Or out.

Consider this a record of intent, if nothing else. I'm leaving it on the counter, straight across from an unlocked door, to be crumpled and tossed away when I return if I'm being a fool.

But if I go missing, whoever finds this ought to head on over to the abandoned house outside of town, the one that's little more than an ash heap. Bring dynamite, and for the love of all things, if you have to shoot, aim for the eyes.

THE REAPING, PART VII

"Monsters," whispers Josiah. Even in his own mind, it is unclear whether he means the great lizard from the story, or the beasts that guide his path.

Perhaps, deep in the dark recesses of his mind, his gaze is turned inward.

Rows of buildings line the streets, all as unblemished as the prison. What wonders, what terrors will each hold that Vulture does not know? Or maybe does not see fit to share.

Josiah meets the mischievous eye of Coyote, the clouded eye of Vulture.

"I wish to leave," he says.

"Where would you go?" asks Vulture.

"Who would take you?" Coyote's question arrives with the barest hint of a snarl.

Tears gather in Josiah's eyes. He refuses to let them fall, refuses to give the beasts the pleasure of breaking him.

When Vulture speaks, his voice is without anger. "I see a long journey. Hot, cramped wagon. Ill-equipped. A journey that should take months, prepared for in a slapdash manner."

"They trusted me," whispers Josiah.

"I see that in their eyes," says Vulture. "Though as the days pass and the stores run bare, those hopeful stares turn to misgiving. Accusatory fingers." Vulture blinks slowly. "'You've doomed us,' says one."

"Ezekiel, my friend," Josiah says through a sob. "God help me, Ezekiel."

"He was the first to die." Vulture's voice comes out flat as the desert floor.

Coyote lowers his eyes.

Vulture continues. "His meaty finger pokes into your chest. Red veins line his eyes, writhing like maggots. His words are riddled, not with mistrust, but with hate. He traps you between himself and the wagon."

"No more." Josiah sinks to the ground.

"Yes," says Vulture. A hint of mania pervades its voice. "You spot the hatchet, the handle sticking up from the jockey box. But you don't grab it, not right away. Why?"

Eyes fixed on the ground, Josiah shakes his head.

"No matter. You stow the information away. Ezekiel presses your body against the wagon, fingers curled into fists, prepared to deal damage. The women shriek, the child cries, your child. The men pay no mind. Ezekiel winds his fist back and—"

"No!" screams Josiah. "Don't say it, don't you goddamn say it!"

His cries wither under the burning sun, transforming into afternoon silence.

"Then you say it." A calm has returned to Vulture's voice.

Coyote sits at attention. Waits.

"I … I buried the hatchet right between his eyes. Before I even realized I'd picked it up, I was swinging it."

"The others?" Coyote looks toward Vulture. The bird remains silent.

"I never seen a man fall so fast. Hit the ground and started twitching. I turned to find Esther, his wife. It wasn't hard. She was screaming. It hurt my ears, made me dizzy …"

"I have no interest in excuses," says Vulture.

"A hand graced my back just then. It felt like my heart stopped. Ezekiel, in his death throes, I just knew it would be, reaching up from the ground to pull me down. One more chance at revenge before he breathed his last." Josiah's voice wavers, eyes flick from Coyote to Vulture and back. "I turned and swung the hatchet once more, hard enough to finish the job. Only it wasn't him. He lay on the ground right where I left him. The blade stuck in my Elizabeth's stomach. Six years old, maybe the hungriest, and she didn't complain once. Trusted her daddy to do the right thing, get us through the mess. And I had to watch her eyes fill with betrayal, even as she gasped for air, flapped her lips to spit out some final words. I told her I loved her. I didn't mean to do it. Even pulled the hatchet free like I could take it back. That only made everything worse."

"The screams," says Coyote. "They must've reached toward the heavens."

"I could barely hear them at first, then they grew louder, like a storm closing in. It was like they were causing Elizabeth more pain. The noisier it got, the more labored her breathing became."

"So, you silenced them," says Vulture.

Josiah nods. Part of him wishes to drop the hatchet, let the sand cover it, but he can't bear to let it go. Not now.

My only protection, my burden.

Vulture steps forward. "Say their names."

"Annabelle, my wife, my God, sweet Annabelle." His voice breaks. "And Esther, Ezekiel's wife. Two sisters cut down with just that many swings." Josiah wipes at his eyes. "I swear it made sense in my head at the time. If I just got some quiet, I could save Elizabeth. So, I made them quiet, Annabelle and Esther. The fastest way I knew how." He lets out a deep, hitching breath. "Elizabeth died in my arms, and it took so long. So godawful long. Shaking and trembling, staring off into the distance. The whole time I held her tight and told her I loved her. She died with a look on her face that said plain and simple, she didn't believe me."

A light breeze whistles down the Buzzard's Edge street. The only sound to split the silence until Coyote begins a new story.

THE ICE MAN

1

Weeks went by as me and Alice counted the stars above our unfinished farmhouse. A peaceful promise of a new life. All that came to an end the day the Ice Man arrived in town.

The fire Noose's goons had set left almost nothing of Taff Ranch except midnight-black cinders and painful memories. It took Alice and me the first couple of days following the death of the notorious outlaw to sift through the ruins for anything useful, then clear away the rubble so we could rebuild from scratch. I'd never built a house before, but Henry Taff taught me part of a man's worth boiled down to what he could accomplish with his hands, and I took that to heart.

Alice taught me it didn't take a man to make big things happen, and she did it all without a word. Just a take-no-shit attitude and the energy of a freshly-branded horse.

Though the town of Buzzard's Edge caught us with the occasional crooked eye, some of its inhabitants showed a quiet gratitude toward us for wiping Noose Holcomb off the face of the earth. Mr. Meyer, the town's cooper and coffin maker, came by and put those burly shoulders to good use, along with a borrowed wagon to haul some wood down from the mountains. Even offered to help get the structure going. I clapped him on the back with a 'thanks, but no thanks.'

Something made me believe this was ours to do.

It's like I said. Weeks passed, and we fed our sweat and toil to the sand. Uncut trees found form beneath Henry Taff's aged set of tools. A little rust along the edges, but they got the job done. When the middle of the day hit and the sun found its peak, we retreated to the shade and gave our bodies a rest. Got to work with our minds.

An incident at the town's largest general store, run by a man named McGregor, kept me away from there. Whether at his behest or just my own caution, I didn't much care to find out.

Instead, I shopped for our necessaries from the only other place that offered such things. Ruby's General. A little hole in the wall run by a woman named Ruby Evans. A few years older than me, she had a soft, mousy quality to her. Almost like she'd grown used to living in the shadows and didn't want to bother anybody. Ruby's stock was wanting, but she always welcomed us with a smile, and didn't seem to look down on Alice the first time I mentioned she couldn't talk. Miss Ruby only got a funny look in her eye and wished us well.

Next time we came by, she slipped a book in with our order. *The Structure of Signs* by a fella named William Stoker.

"What in the world is this?" I asked.

"Well," said Ruby, running her fingers over the cover. "I'm not exactly sure. Took it as part of a trade some months back—reading material is always in short supply 'round here. You know that. I gave it a glance, and it seems like a way to talk just by wavin' your hands around." She shrugged, and a playful smile danced across her lips. "Could be something, could be nothing. But it's yours if you want it."

Alice's eyes narrowed in suspicion. She'd built a little trust with me. The rest of the world? Not so much.

"Ruby, that's a mighty kind thing. How much'll you take for it?"

"No charge, hon. Not if you'll let me know how it works out." A hint of sadness twinkled in her eye as her gaze left mine and swept over the deserted store. "Truth be known, Rory Daggett, I do wonder if anyone but the two of you would miss me if I disappeared tomorrow."

"Hey now, that ain't true." I swallowed, not quite sure what evidence to offer that might support my claim. "You're a dear, Miss Ruby. Don't ever change."

"I'm being stupid." She handed the book over and forced a smile. "I won't change if you won't."

"It's a promise."

Next to me, Alice rolled her eyes, but she didn't look unhappy.

Good as advertised, the book brimmed with pictures of hands and descriptions of how to move them to represent each letter of the alphabet. Other illustrations showed full words and short sentences. Alice took to it right away. Even demonstrated a fair bit of patience with her companion, whose mind worked a little slower. Spelled-out letters gave way to words, and within a fortnight, we had the roots of our own little language. Rudimentary as it was.

This more than pleased Miss Ruby, who lit up every time we came into the store, which admittedly was a bit more often than necessary. The woman appeared to live alone in that closet-sized building and the place never seemed overly busy. Personally, I think Alice liked showing off, and I didn't hate seeing her smile. Tell you, it was damn nice to see that girl wear something other than a grim, bone-straight expression on her face. Each grin, even when they only lasted for a second, put the Arizona sun to shame.

The moon, too.

When the sun set, we always took a moment to admire the day's work, then settled in under the skeleton of the new farmhouse, each sinking into our own stack of blankets, staring up at the night sky. We didn't need no special book to count stars. Had enough fingers and toes to get us to a number that worked well with the exhaustion of the day to put us to sleep.

It was almost sad the night before we planned to start on the roof. We stared up at the darkness overhead, so full of stars, it appeared they might spill over the side if you added even one more. Alice held her hands in front of her chest, palms facing inward, then she flipped them around with a flourish.

All done.

"Yeah, almost. Not quite. We get a roof on this thing tomorrow, and it gets easier from there. Nitty-gritty details. Going to miss this, though."

She closed her right fist, then stuck out her thumb and pinky, rocking it back and forth in front of her chin.

Me too.

"Hey now, just 'cause we got a house doesn't mean we can't camp out front every once in a while. Guess what matters is we got a place to call home, and some well-deserved peace and quiet for a bit. Maybe not a bad idea to stash a few weapons around the place, but Pip, a real place to lie low and figure out what happens next."

Silver wisps of cloud twirled in the sky, wrapping up the stars like a blanket. The slow, subtle movement held my attention for a moment before I realized Alice hadn't answered. No flashy hand signals, not even a tap on the hard floor.

The steady sound of her breathing told me she was asleep. I listened to that soothing purr for a minute or two, then my eyelids gave up trying to keep open.

The sun was barely up when Billy Chambers clopped along on a gelding as old as the dust it kicked up, skidding to a stop in front of our nearly completed farmhouse. The interim sheriff's downcast eyes and tight lips told us immediately that the news was bad.

2

It's an odd thing to invite a man into your home when there ain't no roof to stop the sun pouring in. Still, that's just what we did. Billy Chambers even took his hat off when he stepped through the front door. His eyes crept around the unfurnished parlor, looking for a place to sit. He cleared his throat when he came up empty.

"Don't keep us in suspense," I said. "What can we do for you?"

"Well now, Rory, you'll know I ain't no good at this sorta thing. Just keepin' John's chair warm …" He let out an audible gulp. Nearly a month had passed since the death of Sheriff John Harden by the boot of a steam-engine-sized outlaw named Dorrance. Harden's missing presence still nipped at me. Clearly, at Billy too.

I started to tell Billy to go on, then found myself unable to speak. A little dust in my throat, maybe. Truth is, some people make the world feel a little dimmer when they leave. John Harden was one of those lights.

Billy shuffled his feet, boots clicking along the floorboards, and continued. "Keeping that seat warm until the mayor gets someone better suited to the harder parts of the job, anyway."

Alice chewed her lip and raised an eyebrow at me.

"Billy," I said. "Don't mean to cut to the chase, but it sounds like you're here to haul me in, and honestly, I'm not sure what I've done lately." I flicked a grin his way, hoping it might burn away the tension.

"No. No, no, no. Ain't nothin' like that. Just … Shit, it's just …we had us a murder in town. Sometime last night. A Miss Ruby Evans."

A pit the size of a grave opened in my stomach. Alice shot me a look that told me I must've gone pale and clammy. If Billy noticed, he kept mum.

"There's folks that tell me you and Alice here frequented her little shop. And, uh, you weren't the only ones, but the list wasn't all that long."

He stared at me as if he'd asked a question. I racked my brain, tried to get it to latch onto something.

"I'm sorry." The words dribbled out of me like the last beads of water from a near-dead spigot.

Concern knit across his eyebrows and his voice gruffed up a little. "Sorry for what?"

I shook my head. "She have any family here? What ... Christ, Billy. What'd they do to her?"

His eyebrows drooped. I guess I appeared just pathetic enough to make him lower his hackles.

"Don't think you want me to go into detail. Especially not with ..." He tilted his head toward Alice.

"She can't talk, Billy. She ain't blind, deaf, or simple." Still, maybe he was right. No sense in further traumatizing the little girl who'd been to hell and back.

He nodded. "Guess I can tell you they used something sharp. Not sure what. Barely recognized what was left of her face, if I'm honest."

"Thought you weren't going into details."

"That was me not going into details. Anyway, here's the interestin' part. No clues left behind to speak of, save one. Somebody, presumably Miss Ruby, scratched a couple words into the backside of the counter before they got her. *ICE MAN*. Mean anything to you?"

I made a show of thinking about it, but nothing clicked. An ice man sure as shit wouldn't last long in the desert.

"How do you know she did it? That it wasn't left by the killer?"

"Wood shavings," said Billy. "Under her fingernails."

"What do you need from me?" I asked. The haze from moments before cleared, and a fire kindled behind my eyes. I could practically feel the damn heat. As soon as Billy put his hands up, I knew he'd seen it too.

"Your memory, Rory. Not your iron. Only looking for any kind of lead might help me find this Ice Man. Ever see anyone strange when you paid Miss Ruby your visits?"

I didn't love the way he phrased that last bit. Billy had always struck me as a nice enough guy, but maybe a little slow.

"Any time me and Alice went in, it was just us there."

"Nobody outside that you noticed? Lurking, or what have you?"

I shook my head and crossed my arms. An itchiness to do anything in the world besides stand there and answer questions tickled at the back of my neck. I struggled to keep still.

"She ever mention feeling in danger? Anything like that?" Billy asked.

"Nope. You didn't answer me before. She have any family?"

Billy got a sheepish look stuck on his face, like by firing back a question, I'd deprived him of his fake duties. "That's one other thing I'm trying to find out. She lived alone in the back room. Far as I know, she didn't have no relations in town."

He bit his lip, and I watched his mind work behind his eyes. I had a good guess what the next question would be.

"Rory," he said. "You said she never talked about someone threatening her, but, um, how do I put this delicately? Did she ever mention anyone she might be kicking boots up with?"

"If that was delicate, you ought to stay the fuck away from glass, Billy." I held his gaze for a minute, thought of the way Miss Ruby flashed a smile whenever I walked through that door. The pit in my stomach opened up deep enough for multiple bodies. "No. If she was seeing anyone, I don't know anything about it."

"Shit," he said, putting his hat back on. "I mean, sorry, I just hoped there might be anything you knew to get me half a step closer."

"Well, I'm truly sorry I can't be of more help."

Billy shuffled toward the door, then turned back. "You don't look so good, you know. Listen, I appreciate any help you can give me, but Mayor Harvey laid down some pretty strict orders. Told me to investigate quietly. No blaze of bullets. Not after all them bodies they dug up at your parents' house. It'd make me feel a sight better if you promised you weren't gonna do something … rash."

I do wonder if anyone but the two of you would miss me if I disappeared tomorrow.

I sucked in a deep breath, then said, "I promise." I don't think I lied to him. Not on purpose, anyway. For all I knew, I could look into Ruby's death in a quiet and delicate manner. My version of delicate, anyway.

A bout of relief washed over him, and he simply nodded, then walked out the door. I didn't move until we heard his horse clop off into the distance.

Alice raised her hands, knuckles out, then pinched her pointers and thumbs together twice. I chuckled, thinking how many chances she'd get to use that one.

"What am I doing?" I asked. "I'm going to find out who the fucking Ice Man is and what's his pointy weapon of choice, then I'm going to shove it sideways up his ass."

I waited a beat. "And I'm going to do it without the sheriff's office or the mayor hearing a damn thing. You with me?"

Alice rolled her eyes, then used her right fist to mimic a nod.

3

"Help me with this board, Pip," I whispered.

Two sets of skinny fingers wormed in between my own, ghost white under the glow of the moon. They rested on the fresh wood, only just nailed across the door of Ruby's General to keep scavengers from looting the place.

This time of night, most of the drunks had sauntered on home and the streets would stand deserted for another couple of hours until the sun showed its face. The windows of the bank next door watched over us like empty eye sockets, the tellers having long since counted their deposits and gone to bed. I'd spent many a night sneaking away from the Taffs' ranch, walking aimlessly through town, listening for whispers about Noose and his gang, or just trying to get my mind to alight upon something new.

The chance of us getting caught wasn't nil, but it was as slim as these kinds of odds ever got.

"On three," I whispered, and Alice squeezed the board.

One and two led to three, then we pulled fast and hard. As it tore free, the wood shrieked loud enough to rouse half the town from sleep. We slipped inside and eased the door shut behind us. If anyone emerged with candle and nightgown to track down the source of the hellish squeal, they were too late to catch sight of us.

Once inside, I drew out a match, scraped it across the back of the door. It blazed to life as I swept my gaze across the store. Thankfully, sheets of canvas already hung over each window, thick enough to keep the light from dancing its way to the outside. Either Ruby hung them after closing up shop for the last time, or Billy put them up when he installed the security plank across the front door in an effort to keep civilians away from the scene of the crime.

Hey, maybe Chambers wasn't such a dimwit after all.

I passed the match to Alice and watched her saunter off while I dug out a second.

Ruby's store usually had a dusty aroma. Not unpleasant, more like wooden furniture stowed away for a long time. As I grew accustomed to my surroundings in the dead of night, a new scent overtook me.

Something charnel. A slaughterhouse on a summer day; only the barest hint of that familiar wooden aroma I loved.

I stood there, lost in my thoughts, then flickering flame caught the corner of my eye, intensifying. I spun around, thinking the place was about to go up in smoke, only to find Alice doling out her dying match to four candles stationed on the counter. After she lit the last one, she waved out the match and froze.

It could've been red wax spread across the counter, except none of the candles were the right color. Even without Billy's warning, I knew we were looking at the remains of Ruby Evans. Nothing so grisly as her body left to rot, just the bloodstains that water, cloth, and elbow grease couldn't remove.

I don't know how long I stared before Alice tugged on my sleeve and led me around the counter. She held up a closed fist with only her pinky raised.

I

I didn't need to see her next move to guess the other five letters. Gouged into the back of the countertop, standing a few inches tall:

I might've missed it if Billy hadn't warned us. Shallow as the fingernail scratches went, dried blood had filled them, almost becoming part of the word. A part of Ruby left behind.

My gorge rose, and I fought to keep from heaving my dinner all over the store. Disrespectful wasn't the right word, but it'd do in a pinch.

Alice must've seen me go pale in the flickering firelight because she steadied me with a hand on my back.

"Don't know what I expected to find here, Pip, but this was a bad idea." I shook my head, trying unsuccessfully to clear it, and leaned against a barrel. My arm slid softly through the open top and I jerked it back, studying the cold, gritty substance on my elbow.

"Dirt," I said, brushing my arm off. "Why the hell would she have a barrel of—"

Creak.

Me and Alice went as still as mule deer staring down the business end of a rifle.

That came from the back room.

I thought it but didn't dare speak.

Sign language.

What. Back. Room. Not. Alone.

Every word I'd practiced with Alice over the last month flew from my head like a canary escaping its inevitable death in a coal mine. Even the individual letters went blurry. Instead, I just pointed at the door behind the counter like a fucking idiot.

Alice made Vs with her pointer and middle fingers, then balanced her hands on top of one another and moved the whole setup in a forward circle.

Move slowly and carefully.

The moment hadn't completely stolen all the shit I'd packed in the back of my mind. I drew Henry Taff's revolver, leaving the hammer uncocked. Alice pulled her own gun and did the same. Staying quiet seemed crucial, although if there was someone back there, they likely knew they weren't alone.

Another creak. More insistent this time. Like the first was maybe an accident, but now the person on the other side of the door was attempting stealth the same as us. Shepherding Alice behind me, I took each step with care, hoping against hope the floorboards wouldn't scream and betray our position. Closer and closer, trying to listen for each sound, even as we masked our own. Finally, the door to the back stood within reach. Alice stepped to the side, pulling me with her.

Smart kid. Never stand in front of a door with an unknown on the other side. Good way to wind up with a belly full of lead.

One trembling hand forward, I ripped the door open and prepared to come face to face with Ruby's killer, hands full of knives or some other sharp and deadly tool. The door cried out again as it settled to a halt, sounding more sad than before. The bedroom Ruby had kept was little more than a closet. Any smaller and she might've had to sleep standing up. An old beat-up cot filled more than half the space with a couple crates full of clothes and other goods roughly shoved underneath. No windows or doors to escape from, nowhere to hide so much as a rat.

I let out a sigh of relief and holstered my revolver.

"There's nothing here," I said, and sat on Ruby's bed. "Whatever they killed her over, I hope they're fucking happy. Looks like the poor woman didn't own more than a few shirts and two sticks to rub together." I let my head fall into my hands until I felt Alice touch my shoulder.

When I met her gaze, she gestured toward the floor. A puddle of water only a few inches from my boots.

"Don't that beat all?" I said. "If there ever was an Ice Man, looks like Buzzard's Edge melted him."

4

With Billy's board back in place, we skedaddled home and got inside just as the sun started to intrude through the beams. The roof would wait another day. I couldn't speak for Alice, but beyond being dog-tired, we'd found jack shit of any use in Ruby's store, and it took the wind out of my sails to buckle down and get to work.

Alice checked a dusty corner for scorpions before spreading out her blankets and collapsing there. She touched her pinky to her thumb and held up the other three fingers. A crinkled forehead accompanied the gesture. Not just water, but with a question mark at the end.

I sucked at my teeth and looked upward before I answered. "Could be happenstance. Mr. Chambers spilled his beverage on the way out the door. Something like that."

Twiddling her fingers in search of a response, Alice shook her head. One thing about her, she's a quick study, but always refused to open that book when she got stuck for a word.

"Doesn't ring perfectly true to me, either. But consider the alternative. You really think there's a guy made of frozen water sneaking around Buzzard's Edge murdering people?"

Alice twined her pointer and middle fingers together, then circled them around each while drawing her hands apart. The gesture finished, she sliced a finger across her own neck. A reminder that when you'd faced down a man who dangled from the gallows and refused to die, nothing seemed outside the realm of possibility. Those signs stood for rope and kill, just enough clues to get her part of the conversation across. Kid was downright brilliant with that limited ammunition.

I nodded, keeping quiet. My mind still spinning a little. I guess I must've looked a bit lost, because Alice pointed her two index fingers toward the sky, then dropped them to aim at me.

Go.

"Just thinking," I said. "All evidence to the contrary, I really was convinced somebody else was in that backroom. More than just the sound. Air felt heavy." I shrugged. "Could've been the dead of night weighing down, but ... you know, I don't think so."

She gave me the sign for "same" again. The fist with the jutted-out pinky and thumb shaking back and forth between us. I liked that one. Wasn't just a single word, more like an invisible line linking the two of us and connecting our thoughts.

"Day's a loss, but that's okay. Try again for that roof tomorrow, yeah?"
She nodded and leaned against the wall.

I lay back on the hard wood floor, too bushed to dig out my blankets, and stared up at the starless blue sky, tempted to count clouds.

We'd missed the part of the day where the sun beat down on us directly, though my skin felt a little red. The floorboards digging into my back finally rearranged my spine enough to wake me up, and I greeted consciousness to the tune of two words on repeat.

Ice Man. Ice Man. Ice Man.

Then the boulders in my head started to roll, and an absurd idea clung to the sides. I waited for Alice to wake up. When her breathing hitched, replaced by something softer and a little more sporadic, I knew she was up and ready. Never did take Alice much time to go from out cold to up and at 'em.

"I've got a stupid fuckin' idea, Pip."

I didn't even need to glance her way. Either she was signing "What?" or fixing me with a look that said, "Well, let's have it."

"On the way," I called. "Grab a holster and a revolver. We're going for a ride."

5

Our middle-of-the-night stint as detectives put an odd little delay on the world, setting us out on our tasks around the same time most places were starting to consider closing up for the day. I only hoped our destination might scoff at traditional business hours due to it acting as a less-than-traditional business. Of course, Ghost, my horse, put her attitude on full display, refusing her saddle until she got something to eat.

Alice tapped her foot while the gray mare munched some oats, but the corners of her mouth said that maybe she recognized a little of that stubborn spirit, and that was alright.

"There's a place outside of town. Don't think I've been out there but once. My Pa, not my real one, mind you, but the man who took me in and cared for me after my mom and dad were killed by Noose—"

Alice's eyes widened, and she broke her stare-down with the horse to turn my way. Absolutely wild. Alice and me had met each other less than a few weeks back, yet here we were building a house together, with me taking on what passed for schooling. Still, we barely knew anything about each other.

I chuckled. "Slips my mind every so often how much we haven't gotten around to talking about. Short version is, Noose killed my parents when I wasn't much older than you. Henry and Wilhelmina Taff brought me into their home and raised me." I nodded toward the house, where we kept our meager pile of belongings. Notably the sign language book. "Someday we're going to expand that vocabulary enough for you to tell me why you thought I was killing all those fuckers who ran with Noose. So anyway, Henry Taff used to take the occasional trip outside town to get ice. Maybe once a month. Usually, he left me home with a list of chores, but one time, I got to ride along. Incredible, really. In a world where it's so damn hot every minute of the day, somebody managed to build a place that stays cold."

Alice didn't reach for a sign or make a move. For all I knew, she was familiar with the concept. Sometimes I suspected she just liked to leave me guessing.

"No guarantees we'll find out anything useful there, but it sure as shit seems the next logical step. What do you think?"

A single nod, and it was settled.

Ghost crunched up the last of her oats, then slurped some water, and we were ready to go.

The Blackjack Mountains grew as the buildings on the western edge of town thinned away. A few pairs of suspicious eyes watched us exit the town proper. Thankfully, none of them belonged to Deputy Billy Chambers. Riding behind me on Ghost, Alice offered an occasional squeeze as if to ask, "Are you sure you know where you're going?"

I couldn't really blame her. I'd only been out this way once and to the naked eye, there appeared to be nothing but sand and sun. We pressed on, squinting for the stray piece of signpost that would act as a beacon. Then I saw it. Weather worn and easily mistaken for a dead tree, stunted even before the desert sucked it dry. A small board crisscrossed the top, narrow enough you could cover it with a boot.

Connelly, it would say if I got close enough to read it.

Instead, I hauled Ghost to a stop and looked for something to tie her to. A withered mesquite tree did the trick, though I reckon even Ghost knew it was only ceremonial. By the looks of it, she could've pulled the tree out by the roots if she took a mind.

Alice checked our surroundings while I looped Ghost's reins around a sturdy-looking branch. When I finished, she made circles with her thumbs and pointer fingers, letting the other fingers curl up in sympathy. Then she brought her hands forward.

I let out a laugh. Probably not the reaction she desired, given the way her face dropped.

"Sure looks like nothing, don't it? Ah, but that's the beauty of a little hideaway like this." I beckoned her forward and pushed past the mesquite tree toward another patch closer to that skimpy little sign. Our boots waded through the brush and sand as we traversed a slight incline.

Crunch, crunch, crunch, THUNK.

The last sound caused Alice to shoot back like a frightened mouse.

"Hey there, Pip. You found the front door."

I stepped back and sure enough, a sturdy piece of board the same color as the sand stood out clear as day. Little handle on it and everything. Once you knew where to look, it seemed impossible to miss.

Alice dangled a hand near her holster, and I almost cracked a joke, but given the murder of Ruby Evans, we didn't really know what we'd find on the other side. So, I did the same. Then I shrugged at her, leaned down, and knocked.

A long time passed, or so it seemed, before a gruff, almost inhuman voice came from behind us. "What you want?"

My heart fluttered like a fucking bird, and we spun to meet Brian Connelly. If the Lord grew a six-foot Gila monster, and wrapped it in human skin, it might account for the scowling man who'd snuck up on us.

I raised my eyebrows at Alice. Her hand brushed the handle of the revolver.

"Ice, Mr. Connelly," I said. "What else?"

6

A burst of cold air rushed out as he waved us inside and pulled the door tight behind him. Dim lantern light flickered along the mine-like entrance to the tunnel. It slanted into the hill like we were going down into the basement of the earth. Maybe ten feet or more before it opened into a sparsely decorated room. A couple of chairs and a table matched the wooden planks decorating the walls, Connelly's way to make it feel less like a cave, maybe. Next to a heavy door on the opposite side of the room hung a pair of hooks latched at the center, a cross between a medieval weapon and a set of tarantula pincers. Another iron stake held space for a second pair. I didn't have to catch Alice's eye to assume we were thinking the same thing.

We got ourselves a murder weapon.

"Didn't see a wagon out there." Connelly sat without offering Alice or me a chair, then eyed us with an accusatory glare. Even his voice sounded like something that might come out of a lizard, deep and throaty.

"Well now, I wasn't entirely honest with you out there. I guess it would have been more accurate to say we're looking for information about ice. Not actual ice."

Connelly blinked at me, like he couldn't believe himself in the presence of such a stupid creature.

Undeterred, I continued. "Here about a murder that happened in town. Near on two days ago now."

"Don't know nothin' about that," he croaked. "Ain't been to town in more'n a week. Don't take much interest in what goes on back in Buzzard's Edge, 'cept to get my necessities now and then. The fuck ice got to do with a murder anyhow?"

He glared at Alice, as if daring her to challenge his language. She stared right back at him, eyes as cold as the underground ice supply. Give you one goddamn guess who blinked first.

"Maybe nothing, but uh, we've deemed it prudent to follow all possible leads."

He crossed his arms. Dark dirt speckled the skin all the way to his rolled-up sleeves. "Don't see no star on your chest."

"No, you don't." I hit him with a hard stare and let the implication settle in. His eyes darted toward the holster at my side. "Are you the only person who works here?"

"Yessir. Man it all the day long and retire to a little shack just down the way when the sun goes down. Night gets a little too cold down here for my liking." A beat passed. "That's where I was comin' from when I stumbled across you folks."

While he talked, I wandered the room, taking in the construction. "Fine work, Mr. Connelly. Airtight. Not a grain of sand sneaking in. You build it yourself?"

A sour look crossed his face, and he glanced toward the heavy door. The room where he stored the ice in an even deeper chamber, at a guess. "Built it with my brother, Liam, before the spoiled little shit took off for greener pastures. Haven't seen the fucker in twenty years or more. Good riddance. Great for the planning, useless for the labor. Once the place was built, it was all labor anyway."

"You haven't seen him since?" I asked.

"What I said, isn't it? Set out east. Told me his mighty intellect was wasted in a shithole like Buzzard's Edge. It's like I said before and what I'll soon say to you. Good riddance, Mr …"

"Daggett," I said. "Rory Daggett."

"Jeezum crow." Connelly wiped the ugly look off his face. "You wouldn't be the boy from the train, would you? All them years back?"

I glanced at Alice. She didn't bother to hide her intrigue.

"Yeah. We've met before. Long time ago. I used to come out here with Henry Taff. He took me in after … you know."

"Aye. A good man, that Henry Taff. I miss his banter. Look, sonny. I don't know what use I can be. I wasn't pullin' the shine when I said I go to town as little as possible. And I don't rightly understand how you've connected a killin' with this humble ice business here."

I tilted my head toward the torture tool on the wall. "What do you call those?"

Connelly squinted like he might have misunderstood me. "Those are ice tongs. Only way a man can pick up those mighty blocks stored below." He pointed toward the door on the far side of the little room. "Why do you ask?" The way his face paled in the lantern light made me believe he already knew the answer.

"We think that's what they used to kill the person."

"Lord a'mighty," he said. "That would be a bad way to go if someone took such a mind." He shook his head. "But those haven't left this place, I can tell you that. Especially not in the last week. Don't nobody touch those but me."

Alice held up two fingers, and I nodded her way. "How 'bout that empty stake?" I asked. "Sure looks like there's a pair missing."

Connelly's face drooped, and he studied his dirt-covered boots. "That's where Liam kept his." Silence rushed in to fill the underground chamber. "He took them with him, wherever he went off to."

My shoulders slumped, and I chewed my lip while considering any other question I might ask. A tug at my sleeve and Alice shaped her thumbs and pointers into L shapes. She tapped her forehead with the right pointer, then brought the two hands together.

I nodded. "Mr. Connelly. Humor me a second. You say you haven't heard from your brother in years, but he's still alive as far as you know, right?"

"As far as I know." Connelly raised his head and the corners of his lips twitched. Only slightly, but it was there.

"Bad case of itchy feet, too, sounds like. Don't like to stay in one place too long."

He narrowed his eyes to about the width of a sheet of paper. "What's your point, Daggett?"

"Let's say your brother wandered back into town. If he built this place, surely he could get in here while you slept down the road. My question is, would he be capable of taking a life?"

Connelly didn't say a word, but the look on his face answered my question just fine.

7

"You believe him?"

Alice hauled herself up onto Ghost's back and glanced back toward the icehouse door, or at least the icehouse hole in the earth. She held out a flat hand, palm down, and rocked it back and forth.

"I get that." I hopped up in front of her, giving the reins a little jerk and setting us in the direction of home. "Surprise certainly seemed genuine. But a brother missing in action? Seems a little too easy."

A tap came at my arm and Alice stuck her hand into my line of sight and shaped it into a gun. I thought a minute before understanding struck.

"Law man? Billy Chambers?" A squeeze. One for yes. I clucked my tongue and let the gears turn inside my head. "Might be a little late for that. He made us promise not to get involved, remember? Hard to put him onto Connelly's trail, either Connelly, without walking him through where we been."

No more squeezes, no more hand signals. The silent treatment.

"I'll think on it. If it seems like something we maybe can't handle on our own, I'll bring Billy in." A moment passed with only the light crunch of sand beneath hooves. "I do worry a bit that he hasn't already been out that way. What with the big old clue Ruby left."

As we trotted back toward Buzzard's Edge in silence, I thought of Ruby's smile. Friendly, sure, but was there maybe something more to it? Delight in seeing Alice and being able to bring her words to life. Didn't that smile and those eyes sometimes aim a little higher, though?

"Probably nothing," I mumbled, quiet enough that the words disappeared into the wind before they could reach Alice's ears. Or so she pretended.

The loose desert sand became packed streets and without trying, I realized we'd aimed ourselves into town, rather than toward the farmhouse. Ruby on my mind, her storefront lingered around the corner. What harm in just riding by?

Ghost skirted past the Buzzard's Edge Bank and skidded to a stop, spraying a fresh coat of sand all over Billy Chambers's boots. My eyes wandered up toward his face, which held an unbearable mix of sorrow and anger.

"What you doin' here, Rory?"

My stomach dropped. I'd never heard Billy speak with such venom before. On further inspection, a group of men paced around the entrance to the telegraph office. Christopher Durgin and Niall Dodd, respectively the town's barber and butcher, cut imposing figures, while also drawing attention to the Edge's lack of lawmen.

"Just out for a ride." I nodded toward Alice like that might confirm my story. Honesty must have crept into my voice, because his tone softened the second time around.

"Been another murder."

I covered my mouth and felt my eyes go wide. "Christ, Billy. Think it's the same killer?"

"Same area of town. Just across the way, in fact. Wounds the same as before. Like a sword or some shit. Fuckin' diabolical."

"Somebody we know?"

Billy spat on the ground. "Small town. Everyone knows everyone, don't they?"

"That's not quite an answer."

"Burton."

I took my hat off and laid it against my chest. My gaze tore to the little building across from Ruby's General and the bank. "Not Donny Burton."

"The very same."

Donny Burton had run the telegraph office since before I was born. Must've been up into his seventies. Always had a job for young men willing to brave the frontier and a hard candy for any kid that came in with their adoptive daddy.

"And they ..." My eyes cut back toward Alice. "They did the same?"

"Brutal," said Billy. "Wouldn't advise going in there. Not that you'd need to." That trace of suspicion returned.

"Ice Man?"

"Donny didn't carve nothin' with his dying breath. The fucker with the sharp things made sure of it this time." Billy leaned in and whispered. "One on each temple to put on the finishing touches. Caved in his skull and pierced the man's mind."

Any doubt about the tongs from Connelly's place left my head.

"We gotta be movin' on, Billy." I said it without much weight.

He nodded. "Might consider staying out of this area of town. Unsafe to say the least. And Rory?"

"Yes?"

He dug his heel into the ground, staring at it like he might unearth something of great value. "Be careful, will you?"

8

The stars twinkled over our still roofless abode.

"I can feel you staring at me, kid. Eyes boring into me like Mr. Meyer's drill into a plank of wood."

She made no move to answer.

"I know you think I should've told him. I get it. Another dead body. Nice old guy. And that's on me."

With her right hand, Alice pointed to her right shoulder, then drew the finger across her chest to the left side.

"On us?" I asked. "You know that's not true."

She repeated the gesture with a look on her face that said she'd repeat the line a hundred times if I kept trying to argue. So I quit, letting out a sigh.

"Shit, kid. You're right. Think I'm still coming down from that last bit of bad business. You believe that?" I chuckled. "If I tell you I don't want to involve Billy 'cause I'm afraid I'll get him killed just like John Harden?"

Alice thought for a moment, then made two fists and tapped the right one against the left wrist a couple times.

"Work," I muttered to myself, eyebrows scrunched. "Ah, yeah. It's his job, sure enough. That don't make me putting him in danger any more palatable." I shook my head. "Of course, I'm putting you in danger every time we leave the house. Guess there just ain't no simple solution, Pip. Life is a bit of a motherfucker, ain't it? We leveled an entire group of bandits, left none standing. Not even the ones wrapped up in voodoo or whatever. Just feels like we should be able to take out a lone killer. Some ice collector's little brother. I mean, there's something there. Two people killed right down the street from one another, same weapon. We could totally handle this one, you know?"

My words trailed off and Alice stared at me. Not like she was searching for the right word. More like she'd gotten across everything she needed to and was just waiting for me to talk myself in a proper circle and arrive at the right choice.

Smart little shit, she was.

"Alright," I sighed. "I'll think about it. That good enough?"

And I did. Every which way, trying to get out of running to Billy for help. The sun came up the next day, went down again without us accomplishing much. Alice just stared. Refused to sign a damn thing at me.

The sun came up again.

Went down again.

And it just kept doing that.

Every morning, the blush on Ruby's cheeks came to mind and settled in there.

I do wonder if anyone but the two of you would miss me if I disappeared tomorrow.

Whatever might or might not have been, she deserved justice. I wasn't exactly giving it to her hanging around the homestead with a sulky kid.

I tried to muster the energy to gather up the timber needed for the roof. Alice watched from the shadows. Hot and sweaty from the sun, and tired of all the goddamn silence, I managed about half a stack before I sat down and let out a sigh they could probably hear in the town proper.

"Alright, then. You win. We ain't got to do everything on our lonesome. We'll go see Billy in the morning. Come clean and drop the whole chilly load on his doorstep. Hope he doesn't slap the dunce cap on me, and our information maybe even lines up with something he ain't told us yet. Happy?"

A single knock against the side of the house for yes.

"Fucking decidedly."

9

We set out before the sun came up. Alice didn't need to tell me I looked like a man walking himself to the gallows that morning. A touch overdramatic? Sure, but I felt my shoulders hanging heavier than the revolver tugging at my side.

First thing we built when we started construction on the farmhouse was a stable. Not that Ghost would run off; it just seemed a manageable project to get the wheels spinning and develop some momentum. Damnable thing had a roof, too. That's where Ghost stayed while Alice and I opted to walk into town. Call it penance, or call it what it likely was, a hearty dose of procrastination. Time to let my cogs spin and find their way to some kind of 'ah-ha' moment.

The patch of desert between home and town wasn't particularly large. The silence, on the other hand, made it feel just about interminable. Me and Alice had barely known each other a month, yet I couldn't shake the sense of disappointment coming off her. Relief that I'd finally come around, sure, but maybe if I'd followed her lead, a man would still be alive. Sure as shit sounded like the Ice Man made Donny Burton suffer, and I guess I'd have to live with that.

The closest time Alice came to talking was the arched eyebrow she shot my way when I veered toward Ruby's, taking us the long way to the sheriff's office.

"Relax, it's early. Billy's probably not even in yet. Besides, I'm not backing out of our deal. I just … I don't know. Feels right. Maybe something else I can share jumps out at us along the way."

And I swear I meant that when I said it.

Crunch, crunch, crunch, THUMP.

I glanced back and caught Alice looking pale as a ghost. She stomped her foot a couple more times, and the ground resonated with a very unground-like noise.

Subtle. Quiet. A person walking in the busy daylight hours might not even take notice.

"What in the unholy fuck?" I mumbled. Center of the street halfway between Burton's telegraph office and the Buzzard's Edge Bank, the street made a sound like the entrance to Connelly's icehouse. Less wooden, but cavernous underneath. Kicking at the sand revealed no door, no hidden entrance in the street.

"Sure sounds hollow," I whispered to Alice, taking care like someone might hear. A shine enveloped her eyes, catching the first rays of morning sun. Something between fear and excitement. Suddenly, that look of shame she'd been giving me all morning was nowhere to be found.

A cold sensation trickled down my spine like the Ice Man himself was standing right behind us, as the rusty gears in my head finally caught up with one another. I drew my revolver and eased back the hammer, quiet as possible. Taking a step toward the telegraph office, I said, "I might have to break that promise, Pip."

10

Inside the telegraph office, the fetid odor of blood and death hung heavy in the air. Something else, too. Something sharper and wholly unidentifiable. It prickled at the back of my mind and caused more than a little worry.

Dried blood caked the floor, and I tried, without success, not to picture Donny Burton's last moments when the Ice Man gripped his head between those nasty-looking tongs and squeezed 'til it popped.

The front office where Donny had taken letters and dispatched them for the better part of Buzzard's Edge's existence, at least until last week, was too small to effectively hide anyone or anything. If there was something to be found, I'd lay all my cards on it being in the back room. A business such as this one didn't require much in the way of storage, and it wasn't uncommon for the proprietor to call it a night, lock the front door, and collapse from exhaustion mere feet from the front counter.

My free hand trembled, reaching for the knob to that back room, as I squeezed the handle of my revolver, letting my finger hover near the trigger. Visions of Ruby's General in the dead of night, a sound from the darkness, and the absolute certainty that a weapon-wielding maniac waited on the other side of the door.

The hinges groaned in the otherwise silence of the early morning.

Empty.

A short mattress on a rickety bed frame and a few crates, overflowing with wrinkled clothing, filled most of the space. Larger than Ruby's room, almost comfortable, but hardly decadent.

Alice pinched her fingers together in a circle, then thrust her hand forward and spread her palm flat.

"Don't be so sure of that," I said, stroking my chin. "Help me with the mattress."

We spread out, which still only put a couple feet between us, digging our fingers underneath the mattress and putting chaos to the order of Donny Burton's neatly made, unslept-in bed. As we leaned it against the wall, Alice made a noise. Thinking back, I'm almost sure it was the first I ever heard come out of her. A little bit like a surprised squeak, only not quite so high, rumbling up from a deep part of her throat and escaping from her mouth because that was the fastest way out.

I half cracked a smile, although it promptly fell off my face when I spotted the hole in the floor.

A pitch-black cavity in the ground staring up at us seems genuinely terrifying in theory. At least that would offer a bit of disconnect, some mystery. How deep? Where does it end up? Is the hole occupied?

Shit like that.

The dim flicker of lantern light took a lot of that guesswork away. It was still dark, but I gauged the drop to be about six feet down, roughly the depth of a fresh-dug grave.

I looked up and into Alice's icy blue eyes. If there was anything to read there, I didn't recognize the letters.

"S'pose I'll be the gentleman and go first."

No argument.

I paused with my leg half into the pit and stared at her a moment. "Can't help but notice you're not telling me to stop and go get help."

With a roll of her eyes, she smiled and drew her gun.

Down I went.

II

Unsteady and untrustworthy as it appeared, the bed frame struck me as a better anchor than the little girl who weighed as much as an unadorned coat rack. It wobbled and creaked as I eased myself down but held until my boots silently touched the ground below.

Immediately, I dropped to a crouch, aiming the revolver toward the flickering light, ready to fire at whatever man or beast waited within. Nothing but a warm fire-like glow, painting the walls of a long, low tunnel, carefully lined with the kinds of support beams one might find in a mine. The person who had composed all this clearly knew what they were doing, even if they were in a rush.

After double checking the tunnel's vacancy, I glanced up at Alice and pointed a single finger to the ground. The oh-so-complicated sign for "come on down". Contrary to my slow and painstaking bed frame method, Alice scooted her legs over the side, tucked her revolver into the holster at her side, and dropped into my arms. I lowered her to the ground, and she drew her gun once more.

"Shall we?" I whispered.

The tunnel dipped down a couple of feet, keeping a little dirt over our heads, but allowing enough height to let us walk, even if somewhat stooped in my case. Slow and careful, we made our way forward, eyes open for hiding places in the wall cavities and anything other than dim, straight hallways.

Maybe twenty feet in, a lantern hung off a small iron stake driven into one of the beams. The light teased the way forward, offering nothing conclusive. I pulled the lantern down and let it peek ahead of us and behind. Nothing to show. Not down here.

"At a guess, we're under the street right now. Hell, this might be the exact spot you found the hollow and got my brain working. Now, if I don't miss my guess, I wonder if this path goes to Ruby's. Maybe comes out right beneath her bed, giving Liam Connelly a way to move around beneath the town."

Alice touched her fingers to her forehead, then brought her hand down into a fist, sticking out thumb and pinky.

Why?

"Why indeed? If Connelly needed something from Ruby's General or the telegraph office, walking in the front door and committing murder was a surefire way to get it." I took a few steps into the darkness. "No, I think those are just the starting places. More guesswork, but this whole little maze we got goin' on here likely comes up into another building, and since there ain't been no more murders we know of, stands to reason that's the target. A building he's trying to get into without anyone's notice. So, Pip, what else is right over our heads?"

Alice got that look that meant she was thinking without trying to give anything away, then she went a little rigid. She pressed the four fingers on her right hand against her thumb, and tapped it twice on her open left palm.

"Now we're on the same page. And early morning's a perfect time to commit a robbery. So, what do you say? Guns out and we see if we can stop it?"

She pulled back the hammer in answer and we let the lantern lead us toward the Buzzard's Edge Bank.

12

Another fifteen or twenty feet, and the path ended abruptly. Bless that lantern because without it, we probably would have assumed a dead end. Instead, the meager lighting reflected off a series of iron bars staked into the hard-packed earth. A closer inspection would likely find a similar set back underneath the telegraph office.

I traced them up toward what I assumed was the bank and saw something that frightened me more than any dark tunnel.

Light.

Not so terrifying until you realize that for Liam Connelly to carry out anything resembling a bank heist, his secret entrance would need to remain, well, a secret. Hidden beneath a bed or the like, rather than staring into the dawn's early light.

A pit opened up in my stomach.

"He's up there right now." The whisper hung in the air. "Perfect timing. Bank won't open for a few more hours. By then, he'd be back in one of those other buildings. A couple dozen feet away when the bank manager comes in and sees the mess. Free and clear to get the hell out of Buzzard's Edge as soon as dark sets in and the town hits the hay."

Alice broke an old favorite out of the bag. Drawing a finger across her chest from right to left.

"Love that optimism, Pip. He didn't count on *us.*"

She took that same finger and dragged it across her throat, then raised her eyebrows.

"Kill him?" An uneasiness twisted my stomach. "I don't know. Let's say, not unless we're fearing for our lives. If we can take him drawing breath, we do it."

A nod.

I led the way up the makeshift ladder and tried to poke my head and my gun out at the same time. Not a soul to be seen. Lord knows how Connelly managed to plot out the perfect place to open his hole up, but I found myself directly beneath the counter. In the middle of everything, yet just out of sight. If he could do even a half-assed job of replacing the boards he'd cut through, it'd take a hell of a detective to notice.

I hauled myself up, one-handed, and surveyed the area behind the counter, then froze as a swishing noise drifted out from an open doorway. Confirmation, as far as I was concerned, that Connelly was cleaning the place out.

A light *clink* came from below, Alice following along. I turned back to her and held a finger to my lips. She slid out of the hole in the floor, ears perked up at the shuffle of bills presumably being dropped into a canvas bag.

"Game's up, Liam," I called. Looking for anger, for authority, to make its way to my voice. All I got was a little bit of a shake. The swishing stopped, replaced by the *thunk* of a bag hitting the floor and heavy, intentional footsteps heading in our direction.

His head poked out first, and though I was sure as hell I was going to meet a new face, I damn near fell back down that hole when the Ice Man turned the corner.

"You," I said.

Alice had no words.

"Well, shit," came that grumbling voice, the same one from the ice chamber that sounded like two monstrous lizards fighting over a carcass.

"But your brother," I said. "Liam."

"Don't s'pose there's any reason to keep puttin' the shine on," said Brian Connelly. "Liam's been dead comin' up on twenty years now. Buried under the ice pit to keep his ass from goin' anywhere. Pair of ice tongs right along with him."

The revolver in my hand shook. "But why?"

Connelly let out a dry chuckle, like rocks scraping together. "For the high crime of being an intelligent man. Christ a'mighty, Daggett, who the fuck'd want to sell ice in the middle of the desert? Know what a hearty pain in the ass it is to replenish when the stock runs out?"

I could imagine but kept mum. Alice's eyes flicked between me and her gun. She could raise it and knock him back into the vault with a well-placed shot before he got another word out. Man wasn't much of a threat beyond the nasty-looking ice tongs dangling from his hand. Except I wanted to hear this, needed to hear why my friend Ruby wasn't ever going to smile at me again.

He hocked a great gob of spit right in the middle of the bank floor like it was sand. "Liam was the brains. I wasn't lyin' 'bout that. Fucker could design anything, and I wasn't bad myself." He inclined his head toward the hole behind me. "Saw what I made down there in less than a couple weeks. Hell, the fact that I was even home, getting a bit of rest, when you dropped by, stands as a minor miracle, but a determined man can dig nine feet of tunnel a day. Bet you didn't know that." Connelly let a moment pass, rolling his eyes back into his head like he was reading his own mind. "Liam, though. Always with the ambition, but he'd bounce around from project to project like a fuckin' flea. He said, 'Ice, Brian. It's about perfect. People goin' to need it, hot as this place is' and he was right 'bout that. Designed a chamber that'd keep cool on the most blistering day August had to offer. Bloody miracle. So we built it. And we got the ball rolling. Then he got bored. Said he was tired of the heat, tired of the sand. Wanted to get hisself somewhere east, somewhere north, and try somethin' new."

Alice lowered the revolver, keeping her finger on the trigger. If her intuition was anything like mine, she must've sensed that a criminal doesn't lay his life story on the table, then interrupt it to pick your head up like an ice block.

Connelly continued, something like emotion making it sound like his throat clogged. "We debated back and forth. 'This is home,' I said, and now I realize that was my only argument. 'Fuck what we sunk into this place, and fuck this town,' he said. 'I want more.'"

He stared back and forth between me and Alice, the look of a man seeking forgiveness. Ruby's face popped to mind, and I had none to give.

"I grabbed the tongs off the walls, just meaning to smack Liam upside the head, except the edge caught him right by the temple. I won't never forget that sound, Daggett. A bit like ice crunching, only softer. The fear that cut through Liam's eyes. I won't forget that, neither. You won't remember the sheriff at the time, fella by the name of "Hellfire" Sparrow. He wouldn't have believed it was no accident. I would've been danglin' from a rope before anybody asked for my side of the story." He shrugged. "So, like I said, I buried him under the ice house. Anybody asked where Liam went, and few did, I told them he went east, left me to run the place all by my lonesome. Got to the point where I even began to believe it, and it made me bitter, I don't mind telling you."

Slowly, so as not to draw the ire of those deadly sharp tongs, I took a step toward Connelly, revolver held fast by my side. "Hell of a story," I said. "And I don't doubt the truth in it. But it hardly explains why you're spending a Sunday morning cleaning out the bank. Or why there's two people dead that I do believe you're responsible for. Do you deny it?"

Connelly studied his feet, then answered in a whisper. "I don't. Though, I do wish that weren't necessary. It was gonna be just the first, I swear it."

I gritted my teeth and squeezed the handle of my revolver. "That don't help your case as much as you think it does."

He nodded, a blank look in his eyes. "Guess I got to thinkin' lately that maybe Liam was right. Time to get out of the sand and heat. I knew the business. Maybe get myself somewhere it could thrive. Only I needed money. And ice never brought in enough. Every so often, you see some hardass shove a pistol in the face of one of those nice bankers. That ain't my style. Too much chance of catchin' a bullet for my trouble. Figured I could come at it from underneath. Nobody'd be the wiser. I just needed a place to start. Ruby's General seemed perfect. Right next door to the bank, and nobody ever seemed to go in there. Didn't even mean to kill her, Daggett. It just happened."

"I'm sensing a theme there," I said. "You were just hoping she'd be alright with you turning her bedroom into a mine?"

"Maybe you're right." He squinted my way with a glint in his eye. "How'd you find it, anyway?"

"Street makes an awfully strange, hollow sound when there's a big old tunnel underneath." I shook my head. "What about Burton? You already had a way in."

"Rocky deposit underneath the woman's store. Weren't no good. I guess I could've gotten around it, but that deputy was already pokin' his nose around. Then you showed up at Ruby's that night. Least I suspect it was you. Scared the holy shit out of me so that I spilled my drink and only just got back underground before y'all opened the door." He looked down at the ice tongs and a glint of surprise lit in his eyes, like he'd forgotten he was holding them. "I had to abandon the woman's store and find a new way in, even if it did go underneath the street. Hated to have to do it to Donny, good old buzzard that he was, but time, my friend. Always of the essence."

"Ain't no reason to kill anybody, never mind two. Christ, Connelly. You know we got to take you in, right?"

"Oh," he said, in an absent sing-song manner. "I know you think you do."

Quick as a flash, he swung the tongs and pain exploded in my head before everything went black as a starless night.

13

I woke to the bitter sting of Alice slapping me across the face, the pungent aroma of gunsmoke in the air, and a grateful feeling that Connelly hadn't "accidentally" killed at least one more.

"You get him?"

She shook her head and tapped her shoulder.

"Pleased as I am that you followed my advice, probably would have been okay if you shot to kill this time. Connelly sure as hell wasn't holding back on me."

Her face reddened.

"Sorry, Pip. I didn't mean it. You done good. Maybe even gave us a trail to follow."

I staggered to my feet, the world still spinning a bit. Alice lowered her leg down into the hole and I shook my head, which didn't help with the dizziness.

"Out the front. Unless the tunnel system is more intricate than should be possible with a couple weeks' work, he's only got one place he can come out. Guns out. Shoot to put down like a fuckin' dog."

I kicked the bank's front door off its hinges, and we immediately had eyes on the telegraph office. No need to pop inside. The door stood open with a light trail of blood leading out into the sand. A quick look up and down the street revealed no sign of Connelly. No monstrous man should be able to move that fast. I must've been out longer than I thought.

Alice waggled an index finger my way. For a moment, I thought she was scolding me before I remembered it as the sign for "where?" Rather than answer, I squinted for more signs of a blood trail. A few spots stood out, but mostly the sand had drunk its fill.

"Heading up the street, I think. Out toward the edge of town."

We traded a glance just then, and I wondered if, once again, we shared the same thought.

"The ice house," I said. More like a question than I intended. Alice's nod of affirmation made the notion not seem so wild.

Without Ghost, the trip seemed twice as far. Only the occasional drizzle of blood promised we were on the right path. The "Connelly" sign stuck out, easier to find this time, and the brush that hid the door posed little trouble.

Revolvers at the ready, we pulled up the hatch, ready to blow Brian Connelly's sick mind to Kingdom Come if he waited on the other side. Only the subtle descent underground. Slick with a cool breeze and devoid of sound and life.

Our footsteps tapped on the ground, echoing through the underground chamber. The pale glow of lantern light revealed puddles of crimson. Either the sand in town was greedy that day, or Connelly was losing more blood than before. Hell, maybe Alice had shot to kill after all.

No sign of Connelly in the receiving room and no tongs hung on the wall. That chilly air raced up my spine as I came to the realization there was only one place left he could be.

I nodded toward the ice chamber door. "He's got to be in there. I'll get the door. If you have to shoot, don't hesitate."

Alice didn't give any signs or even nod. Just raised the gun and wrapped her finger around the trigger.

The thick door required a proper wrenching to pull free. A rush of arctic air raced out with a ghost-like mist. With our sight impacted, it gave Connelly the perfect opportunity to burst out and take us down.

Nothing came but cold and quiet.

"Don't move," I whispered, taking a couple steps back to pull the lantern from the wall. Revolver in one hand, light in the other, I poked my head into the chamber. Blocks of ice stacked infinitely deep on a floor so low it seemed to rub elbows with hell. For a boy that grew up in Arizona, it was a staggering and surreal sight. That's not what demanded my attention, though.

Atop the tundra of ice lay the body of Brian Connelly, its fleeing warmth having sunk it a few inches into the top layer. The grisly shoulder wound inflicted by Alice had taken its toll. Lord only knew how he managed to drag himself all the way there. It was the gash across his throat that had done him in, though, no doubt performed by the rust-red ice tongs lying next to him.

I shook my head and pulled the door shut. Dozens of thoughts raced through my mind. Guilt, perhaps. Whether over the murder of his brother, Ruby, Donny, or some combination of the three. Maybe just a hopelessness that Alice and me uncovering his plot had trapped him in the desert and heat forever. So he took matters into his own hands. Turned off the sun and the heat to join Liam.

For good.

Alice's face was unreadable. No pleasure, certainly, but a weary quality that spoke of a kid who'd seen death at least a time too many. I put my hand on her shoulder.

"One more thing," I said. "Then let's go home."

14

"Afternoon, Rory."

So involved was I in laying boards atop the farmhouse that I hadn't even noticed Billy Chambers riding up.

"Or maybe I should call you Roofin' Rory," he said, with a grin so genuine I couldn't help but return it.

I wiped sweat off my forehead and climbed down. "Well, you sure are in a better mood than the last time we spoke."

"Got an update to share with y'all," he said, dismounting from his horse. "On the murders. Seemed to me you took 'em awfully personal, especially Miss Ruby. Thought you might like some closure."

I caught Alice's eyes from her spot in the shade. Same impassive look she had a masterful knack for. I'd have to teach the kid to play poker.

"Yeah?" I asked.

"You acquainted with Brian Connelly?"

I feigned some confusion, then opened my eyes wide. "The ice guy outside of town?"

"Suppose Ice Man might be a better fit. Still workin' on the whys and wherefores, but we got a tip to check his place out." Billy looked flustered. "Anonymous."

"You don't say."

"Found his body in with the ice. Self-inflicted wound across his throat and a note of confession in his hand. Said he killed Ruby Evans and Donny Burton to execute some kind of elaborate bank robbery scheme. Underground tunnels, a whole big to-do. Damn thing of it is, I had the ice thing click a few days ago. Even went to knock on his door." He shook his head. "Nobody home. Guess I know why now. Anyway, conscience kicks in and he leaves a bag of cash at the bank and heads home to get right with God before he goes to meet the big guy. Strangest thing I ever saw."

I raised my eyebrows. "Underground tunnels, huh? What you gonna do with those?"

"Fill 'em in, I s'pose. Don't need any more lawless heathens gettin' ideas." He shrugged. "Just thought you'd want to know. Damn shame. Poor Donny lived himself a long life, but Ruby? I get the sense she had a lot more to offer."

He held my gaze for a moment. Finally, I nodded, not trusting my voice.

"One more thing, Rory."

My stomach dropped, and I waited for the handcuffs to come out.

"What's that, Billy?"

"Connelly had a gunshot wound in his shoulder. Saw that and, for a moment, I thought, I sure do wonder if the man had some help finding his conscience." Billy kicked at the dirt. "Funny fuckin' world, ain't it?"

"Hysterical."

He smirked. "You all have a good day now. Good luck finishing up this project."

"Come a long way on it, but I figure it won't be finished until tomorrow. Guess we got one more night of staring at the stars before we cover them up for good."

Billy rode off, and I joined Alice in the shade. She hooked her two pointer fingers together, then flipped her hands and did it again.

"Hold on. Wait. Don't tell me." I chewed my lip. "Friend, right?"

A single nod.

"Yeah, maybe." I chuckled. "And maybe not as simple as I used to think, either."

With a groan, I hauled myself up. "Come on, kid. We got a ways to go, but we're closer than ever."

THE REAPING, PART VIII

The world is dark.

"Open your eyes, Josiah. Our journey is nearly at an end."

Vulture's disquieting voice.

This story had stretched on longest of all. So long that Josiah daydreamed of Rory Daggett—a better father to Alice than Josiah ever was to Elizabeth, a mythic figure to the town of Buzzard's Edge—and allowed himself to hope everything from the abandoned wagon, doused in blood, to the talking animals, to his confession, had been a dream.

Josiah opens his eyes.

Hot breath trails across his neck as Coyote latches onto his collar and drags him off the ground.

"Just about there," says the beast. "Got a question, though. How come you didn't take the wagon? Chose to walk all this way?"

Josiah doesn't answer, only marches forward, prison guards on either side.

"Isn't it obvious?" Vulture lets out a croaking noise. "Penance."

Past the schoolhouse, he spots the open desert. Could he make it before they stopped him? The trio halts at the base of the schoolhouse stairs, the notion of escape still flickering in Josiah's mind. His legs feel heavy.

"This is the first place you brought me."

"Like a big ol' circle, ain't it?" Coyote's tone contains a playful quality which its eyes fail to match.

Josiah swallows. "You said there were people. That I'd meet everybody before the journey ended."

Vulture flutters to the top of the steps, stares down stoically. "Everyone is dead, Mr. Dennis. Those creatures that chased off Violet Conway left no one alive, left the town uninhabited."

"So …" Josiah chews his lip. "Every other story you told is destined to happen somewhere, some *time* down the line? Rory Dagget maybe hasn't even been born yet?"

"That is the barest truth of it," says Vulture. "But there is a hinge."

"A hinge," repeats Coyote. It sets on its haunches, stationed between Josiah and the horizon.

No accident, he thinks.

"It has been months and months since the first story took place," says Vulture. "This land demands blood. The last sacrifice happened too quickly. It drank its fill greedily, then forgot the taste. It falls to Coyote and I to trigger its memory. Only then will Buzzard's Edge draw more people to its heart."

"That's why you told me all those stories?" asks Josiah, a confused valley forming between his brows.

Vulture twists its beak into something like a grin. "We filled you with those stories, that you might take them back to the earth."

The light breeze reappears, dragging grains of sand across one another. A scratching sound like the dry husks of dead insects rubbing together.

Sweat dampens Josiah's forehead and his leg muscles coil. He flicks his gaze toward the open desert once more.

I could make it, he thinks.

Coyote shakes its head as if it can read Josiah's thoughts, then paws at the ground.

If not away from town, perhaps deeper into town.

"George Holcomb and Merella," says Coyote. "Elijah Sparrow, Andrew and Wes, Thaddeus Locke, Nola Betts. Even Rory and Alice."

"None of their stories can happen without a reminder of what keeps the land alive." Vulture cocks its head toward Coyote, and Coyote turns away. "A sacrifice."

The hollow in Josiah's chest thrums, his heart beating hard enough to lead a prison break. His legs turn to water beneath him.

Run, screams a voice inside his head.

He turns to flee and a mass of fur and muscle barrels into his back, knocking him off his feet to send him skidding through the sand. As fast as Josiah can flip over, Coyote presses its paws down on Josiah's chest, lips pulled back in a savage snarl. He squirms to escape Coyote's hold but finds himself pinned tight.

Was the beast this large before?

Desperation claws at Josiah. "P-please. Aren't sacrifices supposed to be innocent? You know my story, Vulture, Coyote. You know I've done terrible things."

With a soft *thump*, Vulture lands beside Josiah. "This land drinks blood, Josiah. It feasts on misery. Above all else, it craves depravity. Coyote and I could not have chosen a more worthy sacrifice."

Josiah makes another effort to wriggle free. Coyote's paws only push him further into the ground, pressing down on his ribcage with a force to rival the weight of a horse. Blood pounds in Josiah's ears, but he swears he can hear the crack of bone in his chest.

My eternal reward. My torture.

"When the town is thriving once more," Vulture whispers, "We'll make sure the people remember your name."

The bird winks with its milky eye, then nods.

The last thing Josiah Dennis sees before Coyote rips his throat out is Vulture's jagged beak racing toward his eyes.

When It's All Said and Done

"I don't know much, but I know it shouldn't be black." Mort wrinkled his nose in disgust.

Jack kept his mouth shut, choosing instead to study the toothpick with a lump of gooey black substance hanging off the end.

Mort shook his head. "I don't confess to keep as clean as maybe I should, but I daresay you won't find anything in my mouth looks like a piece of wet coal." He stood and his knees let out two loud rifle cracks.

The bigger man, Jack, remained knelt beside the body. "Weren't no gold in there," he said with a shrug and a sigh.

"And you thought his fuckin' mouth would be the best place to look?"

"Nothin' in his pockets." Jack shrugged.

"You volunteerin' to check up his ass?"

"Speaking of ass, it's starting to stink in here. I say we get rid of him." Jack chewed on his lip. "Don't know what we expected. He was a simple tradesman. Nobody like that got riches socked away."

Mort eyed the body greedily. "Plenty of people out here sittin' on secrets."

"Mmm. You sure you heard Farrell right? That there'd be gold?"

Shifting uncomfortably, Mort said, "He said somethin' of value, I believe. We'd know it when we saw it. What's more valuable, or obvious, than gold?"

Jack fixed him with a hard look. Not judgmental, but the kind of stare that makes a man turn inward and examine what they really think.

"I guess he coulda meant somethin' else. Don't think he intended we oughta bring half a big black booger, anyway." Mort cleared his throat. "You know what we gotta do, right? Go talk to Farrell. Try and get ourselves squared away."

Jack let out another sigh, this one a real doozy. "Seems inevitable, don't it?" He patted the corpse's pockets once again. Not too thoroughly, but enough to catch any stray gold nuggets worth catching. Evidently satisfied, he stood, towering over Mort, and glanced toward the window. Jack flicked the black-gunked toothpick across the room where it landed with a sound like a tiny gunshot.

"Shit's sake," said Mort. "What the hell was that?"

Wide-eyed, Jack watched a plume of smoke wisp into the air from the toothpick.

"Don't rightly know, but I suppose we best be going. Moon's in a place makes me think ridin' him out and leavin' him in the desert might be the best option. If we bury him here, we might still be at it when the sun comes up." Jack's gaze glided toward the corner of the shop. "Could put him in one of those coffins, I guess. Other room's got tools, we could ..."

Jack shifted his hand back and forth in a sawing motion.

A small shudder passed over Mort. "Nah, desert's okay by me. Besides, you see that design on the wall? I can live without goin' back in there."

"Looked like a big eyeball carved into the wood. Gave me the willies," said Jack.

"You ain't wrong," said Mort. "Willies aside, probably best to get the evidence out of town. New sheriff used to be a detective; figure he's got a mite more goin' on upstairs than the last few men to wear the badge."

"Got to imagine he's still busy sorting out that mess from up in the cavern." Jack blew a breath out his nose. "Desert it is. Wrap him up, then, Mort."

"Fuck you, you wrap him up. I'll get the horses. Remember what happened last time your big ass tried sneakin' out in the dead of night?"

Jack spat, eyes never leaving the corpse. "If I ever forgot, I s'pose you'd be there to remind me."

"Just lucky that girl's daddy was useless with a rifle. Man couldn't hit an ox if it turned sideways for him." Mort cracked a grin, then slapped Jack on the shoulder. "Back in five, my friend."

Silent as the onset of night, Mort slipped down the street and untied their horses from in front of the Saloon at the End of the World. Not wise to leave them dawdling outside a building where you planned to take a man's life. Hooves barely scraped the ground, so lightly the jostle wouldn't have woken a sleeping infant. When he returned to the dead man's place of business, Mort let his knuckles dance across the wooden door in a practiced rhythm; a comforting ostinato that told Jack it was only his partner and everything was hunky dory.

Jack eased the door open, blocking the flickering candlelight with his massive frame. Slung over one shoulder was a moldering tarp with a large pair of boots hanging out the end. He stepped out into the moonlight and laid it over the back of his black-and-white gelding with surprising gentleness.

"We good?" asked Mort. "Ready to commit Mr. Meyer back to nature?"

"I reckon." Jack heaved a leg up and over his horse, the more sturdy of the two, and the only one equipped to carry his bulk. "Wasn't no gold up his ass, neither."

Mort raised an eyebrow, studied Jack for a moment. "Jesus Christ, I can't even tell if you're bein' funny or not."

Instead of answering, Jack gave the reins and gentle tug and led the way out of Buzzard's Edge.

Jack snored like a steam engine rumbling down the tracks. No whistle to warn that the fucker was about to run you over. The harsh bellows echoed off the walls of the barren little backroom at the saloon.

They'd returned around daybreak, covered in sweat and grime, to the lingering stench of booze and unwashed bodies, as well as a note from Julie, the hot-headed angel who ran the show anytime Mort stepped out.

Tommy O'Shea heaved his guts behind the piano and Old Bill Gardner started another fight while you were gone. I'll take my thanks in cash, if you please. - Jules

With a smirk, he'd crumpled up the note and followed Jack to the back room to try and squeeze in a few hours' rest before paying a visit to Farrell.

It's always fucking cold in here, thought Mort as he sat awake in the dark.

He'd taken over the Saloon at the End of the World after the deaths of the previous two owners, scoffing at the name at first, then allowing it to grow on him, if only because after the events of the last year or so, maybe Buzzard's Edge needed a little consistency. Part-time barman, part-time bouncer, Jack often slept in the back room. Most of the other staff wouldn't set foot in there.

Not even Jules.

Mort often wondered whether that was down to experience or hearsay. Unfortunately, voicing that question was a good way to lose a pretty barmaid.

A table and a few chairs sat in the corner, dried blood crusted on their surfaces. No matter how hard a person scrubbed, they refused to come clean. Trying to get rid of the stains only filled the air with a strong, coppery stink.

"Nothing here," whispered Mort, and he wanted to believe it. "Just a gaping hole."

Jack's snores stopped so abruptly that for a moment, Mort wondered if he'd up and died.

"What'd you say, Mort?" Jack asked through a haze of sleep.

"Nothing," said Mort. "Nothin' at all."

No windows in the room to let him guess at the time of day, Mort climbed to his feet and opened the door to the saloon. Rays of sun trickled in, little by little, as if afraid to touch the shadows in the backroom.

"A little past midday, by the look of it." Mort sucked his teeth.

Jack's eyes went wide as he stepped into the saloon. Not fear, only surprise. The cold, the scent of blood, and the sense of being watched never seemed to bother the big man. Yet when he spoke, his voice contained a rare hesitance. "Sure you still want to pay a visit to Farrell?"

"I'd say we'd better. And sooner than later."

"What if we asked him to come here?" Those nerves again.

Mort's eyes narrowed. "Alexander Farrell ain't the kind of guy that comes to a whistle. Somethin' wrong?"

Jack opened his mouth to speak, then quickly shut it and shook his head.

"Look, I don't mind saying I'd rather not go alone. You with me?"

Jack nodded. His mouth, straight as a cactus spine, gave him a resigned and weary look.

"Well then, pal," said Mort. "Ready to go visit the competition?"

Past the Sheriff's office, straddling the town line at the outskirts, the Scarlet Revolver cast a thin shadow halfway across the street. Two stories tall and far more refined in appearance than the internal goings-on deserved, it made the Saloon at the End of the World seem like a hovel.

Jack glanced up at the second story. His cheeks darkened a shade, though Mort saw only an empty window, curtains shuffling in the meager breeze.

"I'll go in if you tell me so, Mort, but it's not my favorite place."

Mort slapped him on the back. "Relax, pal. Sun's still in the sky. The joint won't be jumpin' yet, and you never know who we might, or might not, run into."

"Kinda what I'm afraid of," muttered Jack.

"Just try not to touch anything. I don't know as I can keep paying you if you bring some sort of disease back to the saloon."

The crimson hue in Jack's cheeks vanished, replaced by a dingy maggot white. He nodded and slumped his shoulders.

"Buck up, pal," said Mort. "Let me do the talkin', and don't let Farrell see you sweat."

Inside the batwing doors, a small, modest room greeted the men. Unadorned walls, free of clutter or dust, narrowed in toward a counter just the right size for a single person.

Jubilant music rattled the paper-thin walls, the hired performer not playing the piano so much as punching it like a prizefighter. Discordant harmonies formed a poorly conceived veil to keep passersby from hearing the screams of ecstasy drifting down from the dozen rooms that branched off the main parlor.

"Help you, gentlemen?" A stern-looking older woman scowled out from behind the lone piece of furniture, raising an accusatory eyebrow and looking like she'd rather do anything than take care of Mort and Jack. She'd allowed Mort back before but seemed to revel in pretending not to remember him.

Mort smoothed back his hair and kicked Jack in the side of the boot, simultaneously shooting him a knowing look. Jack took off his hat and all but made it disappear, wringing it in his massive hands.

"Why, yes, you can, Miss Agatha."

The woman's eyes narrowed, and creases appeared at the corners of her mouth, like she couldn't stomach her name dancing across the tongue of such a low creature.

Mort cleared his throat and continued. "Looking for Mr. Farrell." He leaned against the counter. "Urgent business matter we'd like to, uh, get straightened out. He in?"

Miss Agatha let her eyes rove up and down Mort and Jack, searching for any flaw that might allow her to deny them admission. Seeming to see nothing that justified throwing them out on their asses, she sighed and waved to a door behind her.

"Thank you, mon chéri." Mort offered up his most charming smile, receiving only a stoney glare from the matron in return.

The moment they stepped through the next door, Jack winced, overcome by the noise. Undesirables surrounded the bar, screaming out their orders, and speaking over each other the way men well into their cups will do. Bangs emanated from every corner of the room, both in the literal and figurative sense, and Mort counted more bare breasts in five seconds than he had in the last thirty years of his life.

He placed a hand on Jack's shoulder and found the big man shaking.

"A whole town travels north, starts shootin' and stranglin' one another 'til you're down a quarter of the population. One would think it'd be a little less crowded around here."

"Sure," said Jack, eyes darting nervously around the room.

Mort pushed him forward, past the bar, the piano, the ruffians, and all the exposed skin a man could desire, until he caught sight of a table tucked away in the corner of the room, hidden by shadows. A decorative tablecloth flapped over the side, held in place by half a dozen plates of unfinished food, finer fare than anything a casual drunk could order at the saloon located a pistol shot down the road. Moving among the boiling shadows sat two men whose girth told of their prominence and ability to satiate their every need.

"—tell you, I don't think it'll be a problem," said the man on the left. A razor-thin beard looped around his mouth, ending before it could grace his cheeks; so neat, it could only be the result of a daily trip to the barber. Alexander Farrell.

The man on the right nodded, drumming his meaty fingers on the table. A smirk spread across his face, the kind only the man who runs the show can summon. "A little bit more on his game, sure, but it's not like any of the previous sheriffs were fools."

Mort cleared his throat. "Mayor Harvey. Mr. Farrell."

The two men stopped their chatter, freezing in place like blocks of ice. Mayor Harvey's face dropped, eyes locked on Jack. He recovered so quickly, Mort might have missed the slip if he hadn't been staring.

"Jackie boy," said the mayor, eyes glowing with something unidentifiable. Jack shrunk back, unable to hide himself behind Mort.

Mort's throat went dry, and his eyes darted back and forth between the two men. He'd only ever come to the Scarlet Revolver alone, but seeing Jack and the mayor side by side ...

Was there a little resemblance or was his imagination off to the races?

"Now, don't slink away, kid," said Harvey. "It's been a long time. Too small a town to miss seeing your own brother. Am I right?"

Brother.

Mort tried to blink the shock off his face. Thankfully, no one was paying attention to him.

"Been busy," mumbled Jack.

"Speak up, Jackie." Mayor Harvey shot a wink toward Farrell. "Always was a mama's boy."

"What brings you gents here?" asked Farrell. He wore a grin like a bank robber wears a mask.

Mort shuffled his feet, letting his eyes dance around the room. "Well, Mr. Farrell, come to follow up 'bout that, uh, matter from our last visit."

If Farrell remembered their previous conversation—the one about a little murder for hire and some item retrieval—his face gave nothing away.

"That right?" he said, leaning his head to the side and cracking his neck. "Mr. Mayor, I don't mean to be rude. Neither, I think, do these two gentlemen, but perhaps we could continue this conversation at another time?" Farrell seemed to add another sentence with his eyebrows, but Mort couldn't guess what the unsaid words might be.

"And girls?" said Farrell. "Maybe go make yourselves useful somewhere else."

The cloth hanging over the table's edge began to ripple before a pair of topless girls slinked out from underneath. Red with sweaty hair matted to her forehead, the first girl wiped a hand across her mouth, lowered her gaze to the floor, and vanished among the rabble near the bar. The second girl smiled and shot a wink at Farrell. He turned his head away, and the grin fell from her face.

Mayor Harvey stood, making the dishes rattle across the table and tucking his dick away before buttoning up in a pitiful stab at modesty. "You know where I'll be," he said, slipping out from behind the table. He brushed past Mort without a word, then stopped to lay a hand on Jack's shoulder. Beneath his older brother's grip, Jack looked like a little kid. "And you know where I'll be, as well, Jackie. Come on and see me sometime. We'll find you something a little more … dignified to earn a buck, eh?" Harvey squeezed, drawing out a pained grimace on Jack's face, then ambled off toward a staircase and disappeared up to his rooms.

"So," said Farrell, spreading his arms across the backs of the surrounding seats. His sharp voice made Mort jump. "Is it done?"

Mort let his gaze hover toward one of the open seats. Farrell made no move to offer it.

"It's done," said Jack. Not a trace of emotion to be found in his voice. A bead of sweat dripped down the side of his head, and his body language told of a man who just wanted to go home.

"Can't be that easy," said Farrell, "Because if it was, the two of you wouldn't be here, not with empty hands anyway, interrupting my business and ruining a perfectly good blowjob."

"Ah, no sir, s'pose you're right." Mort tried to meet Farrell's eyes but failed to hold them.

"So, get to the fuckin' point before I decide to rope in the closest body to finish what that little girlie started."

"See, it's like this, Mr. Farrell. We snuck into the cooperage, middle of the night and all, tried to catch Meyer by surprise. Don't think he ever went to bed, though. Dressed like it was midday, and we sure didn't catch him sleeping. I pointed my pistol right between his eyes, and it might have been a shoe for all the fear it inspired in him. Big fucker cocked an arm back to put my lights out. If it wasn't for Jack here, sneakin' up behind him with a length of rope, I guess—"

Farrell held a hand up, no longer wearing that fake smile. "I don't give a fuck. I don't need details. What I need, is to know why you're here. If our agreement has been carried out. If you have something for me."

"Well, it's—"

"If you tell me what it's like again without telling me why you're here, I'll have your testicles and eyeballs swapped."

Jack swallowed audibly. Mort licked his lips, searching for the words. "You said Meyer had a stockpile of gold, we could split it if we took care of him. 'Cept there wasn't more than a few bucks in the whole shop."

Farrell covered his mouth as if trying to suppress another threat. His eyes crawled back and forth between Mort and Jack before he lowered his voice and spoke. "First off, I never said shit about gold. Second, I'm trying to figure out whether you came here to accuse me of being a liar or shake me down. I can't say I care for either. So, Mortimer, one more time. What are you trying to say?"

Throat constricting, Mort heard his voice take on a whinier tone than he would've liked. "Nothin' like that, sir. We just want to get paid for our work."

Farrell continued to stare. If his eyes had narrowed any more, they would have looked like mouths. Mort's balls retreated up into his stomach. He tapped his foot nervously, waiting for the hammer to fall.

"Mortimer Everlie. Jack Harvey." Farrell's voice was dead even. He could have been ordering a steak. "Do I look like a man who allows sniveling cunts to walk into his establishment and accuse him of being a cheat?"

Mort's knees shook, and warm piss threatened to dribble out of him. *Run*, his mind cried, but not a single part of his body promised obedience.

Farrell lifted a hand from under the table and let a revolver clatter onto the table. He watched Mort and Jack, as if daring them to fight or take flight.

Then he laughed.

His grin slithered back onto his face. It still had the look of a man who couldn't comprehend why people lift the corner of their mouths into that particular shape.

"Mea culpa, gentlemen," he said. "Even a man with as many demands as me needs to have his fun from time to time."

Confusion swirled in Mort's mind, though a relieved whoosh of air passed over his shoulder. It sounded as though Jack had held his breath throughout the whole exchange and only now dared to let it free.

"I … I guess I don't understand, sir," said Mort.

"I mean, we'll get you paid." A shadow passed over Farrell's face, stealing some light from that false grin. "But only after you come through. Maybe I wasn't clear before. There's an item in Meyer's store—has to be there—and it might seem strange, even out of place, but it would mean a great deal to me. Make me feel safe. A man like me? We don't always feel safe, not even in the belly of our own place of business. Sometimes gunpowder and bullets just don't do the trick. A man needs something … more. You gents have the ability to make my dream come true. Imagine the rewards that might come with such a thing. Now, you said you searched the store, but Meyer was a wily one, always was a little more than met the eye to him. Wouldn't you say?"

"Sure." Mort had only met the man a few times and found him perfectly pleasant. Hadn't relished the idea of murdering him in cold blood, but hey, business was business. "What … what's the item look like?"

"Believe me when I say you'll know it when you see it but be careful. It can be … volatile." Farrell rapped his knuckles on the table. "Tell you what, I want you to head on back to Meyer's store. Make it at night, and look sharp, in case the law is pokin' around. Promise me you'll give the place a real thorough once-over—hatches in the wall, hidden basement, the works. Bring back anything interesting you find and we'll take care of you."

Mort nodded slowly, catching something snake-like in Farrell's eyes as he said the last words. He glanced at Jack, but his friend—*the mayor's goddamn brother*—stood still as a statue, barely daring to breathe.

"Appreciate that, sir," said Mort. "We'll go through the place real careful-like. You can bet on that."

"That's exactly what I'm betting on, Mortimer. And Jack?" Another shadow passed over Farrell's face. "Listen to your brother. I don't give a shit what kind of grievance you got with him. He can set you up so's you don't have to pick up scraps anymore."

Jack nodded, eyes on his boots.

Red-hot rage bubbled up in Mort, threatening to make his fists clench or lips sneer. By the grace of some deity or another, he managed to stifle it.

"Thank you again, Mr. Farrell." The words tasted acidic, and Mort turned and strode back toward the entrance before the bitterness crept out of his mouth. He glanced back once before slipping through the door that led to Agatha. Only the shadowy corner remained.

"Don't make me wait, boys." Farrell's words drifted from the darkness, deadly serious, and yet almost lost to the clamor of the Scarlet Revolver.

Mort and Jack sat in the backroom of the Saloon at the End of the World, door cracked to a slit, letting in a touch of light and enough rowdiness to keep them from bathing in the awkward silence. Jules had stared daggers as they slipped inside, but she'd hold her own out there, and Mort would empty his pockets in apology once they collected from Farrell.

Outside, the sun had dropped below the horizon, but the night was still too young to try their luck at Meyer's. Across the room, Jack scraped his knuckles against the bare floor, ticking away the seconds until it was time to leave.

"You gonna talk to me?" asked Mort.

A few more dry scratches, some heavy breathing that spoke of frustration. Not quite a sigh.

"Why didn't you tell me your brother was the mayor, Jackie?" He cleared his throat. "Jack. Sorry, pal. Wouldn't have dragged you along if I knew you was gonna button your lips and act like someone snatched the wheels off your wagon."

Mort grinned. Even in the dim light, he could tell Jack didn't return it. "Shit, you never even gave your last name when you first set foot in the saloon. How'd I miss that?"

"You never asked," said Jack, voice solemn as a tombstone.

"You serious right now?" asked Mort, eyebrows creeping up toward the brim of his hat.

"He ain't a good man, not like he pretends to be." Jack's words came out soft and small, barely enough conviction to get them across the room.

"Well, I don't mean to judge none, but he does live above a whorehouse." Mort picked at his nails. "Not that there's anything wrong with supporting those ladies. Just sends a certain message, that's all."

The clamor of clinking glasses and half-shouted speech drifted back in to fill the lull in the conversation.

"He killed our mama. Bet you didn't know that."

Always was a mama's boy.

Mort swallowed. "Jeeeeesus. Sure as shit didn't. So, tell me, how's a man like your brother get to be mayor?"

"A man who'd kill his own mother?" asked Jack. "I'd say that kind of man could become anything he wanted, short of decent."

"I'll say."

Jack scooted closer. "Daddy was a woodworker—ain't that the peak of irony? Had a little shop out of our spare room. Kept to himself, and when he did come out, never had a kind word for either us or Mama. One day he stepped outside, shook his head at me like I was some kinda unwanted animal, and wandered off into the desert. Empty-handed, like he'd just had enough of this life. Maybe got sick of this town. Moses wasn't more'n—"

"Moses?"

Wrinkling his eyebrows, Jack said, "My brother."

"Shit. I thought his name was Mayor."

Jack cracked a grin that seemed to bring a little more light into the room. "Anyways, he was 'bout eleven or twelve, me about eight, when that man left us all alone with Mama. She did her best, workin' odd jobs tryin' to put food on the table for her boys. Only it were never enough, Mort."

He raised his eyebrows as if trying to pass along an unspoken part of the story.

When Jack spoke again, there was a hardness to his voice. "Moses, good son that he was, started workin' a few years later. Down one of Farrell's mines. Grew bigger n' stronger than you'd expect from a twelve-year-old. Brought home some good coin too. Too good. Fair bit more than a mine worker usually earns."

Mort sat forward. "And you think maybe he was doin' something for Farrell on the side?"

"More than think," he whispered, tapping his knuckles on the floor again. "Got to the point where Mama didn't have to break her back no more. Moses sits her down with this 'Ain't you proud of your boy' attitude, 'cept she ain't. Virginia Harvey wasn't no fool, even if she did raise one or two."

"She ask him where the money came from?" asked Mort.

Jack shook his head. "Not then. Just got up and walked away."

Tap, tap. Tap, tap.

"Next time she brought it up was when she found his gun." Jack's voice pitched higher, and Mort guessed the man's throat had grown a little tighter. "All the stupid asshole had to do was say one of the other miners had given it to him. That he only used it for pluggin' critters. Better yet, that he'd never used it at all." Jack bit his lip. "Nope. Instead, he comes clean, mostly clean anyway. Says that gun is the only reason she gets to sit at home on her ass all day. Mort, I thought she'd yell and scream, maybe haul off and slap Moses, but she only looked at him. Not a bit of anger in her eyes. More like disappointment, and when she spoke, it wasn't but a whisper. Said, 'I'd rather work my fingers to the bone than have my oldest son out there partakin' in duties what compromise his eternal soul.'

"Then she slid her hand over the gun. Didn't take it, just covered it up like her hand was big enough to make it disappear. Only Moses reached for it, too." The next words crept past tears and barely made it out. "And I just bet you can guess the next part."

"It went off," said Mort.

Jack nodded and, once more, silence permeated the back room. For all the stock Jules put into that room being haunted, Mort never believed it, never felt it. Not until that moment.

"Forgive me, friend, 'cause this story's got an awful lot of woulda's and shoulda's. I told you Moses killed our mama, and it wasn't on purpose—I know that—but that don't change what happened." Jack crossed his arms. "The moment Mama toppled off her chair, eyes dull before she even hit the floor, that was when Moses coulda tossed the gun away and tried to make a change. Instead, he pointed it right between my eyes. 'Swear to me you ain't gonna tell a soul, Jack.' I raised my hands and looked down at Mama. Blood puddled out from underneath her, creepin' toward my boot. I shook my head. Guess Moses ain't the only stubborn Harvey boy."

Jack swallowed with a dry click. "He cocked the hammer back. The gun trembled in his hand. Deep down, I didn't think he'd shoot me, but he'd already caused one accident, hadn't he? Sometimes I wonder if he had the same thought, 'cause he lowered the gun and let out a sigh. 'I ain't gonna shoot you, Jackie,' he said, 'but if you tell Sheriff Sparrow 'bout all this, the extra money, there's people that might be more carefree with their trigger fingers, and I can't stop 'em.'"

"Think Moses was lyin'?"

"Not for a second. I told him to go. That I'd keep my mouth shut, but I didn't ever want to see him again. Know what that fucker did? He grinned. Almost like he knew back then he was about to put himself in a position that'd make stayin' out of my life impossible."

"Shit," said Mort.

"And I let him."

"The hell you did."

"It's true, Mort, and the worst fuckin' part? He was right about it all. Look at me, now. How'm I gonna hold a grudge when the only way to get ahead in this fucked up world is to do things that compromise a man's eternal soul? It ain't been a whole day since we killed a man for a few bucks."

"And didn't even get those few bucks."

Jack narrowed his eyes and shot Mort a look that said, *that ain't the point and you know it.*

Slinking his shoulders like a whipped dog, Mort said, "So what you wanna do? Shameful as it seems I'd take the financial hit, only Farrell expects somethin' brought by his place of business. And, uh, I got a guess who your brother mighta been talkin' about when he said there was people he worked for who might hurt you."

"I got the same goddamn guess, I'd wager." Jack let out a low sigh, long as a train whistle. "Don't see as we got any other choice."

Mort nodded. "Maybe we have us another conversation when it's all said and done. See if we can't find a way to make the saloon a little more profitable or land somewhere else, maybe."

Jack looked up at the prospect, eyes shining with something like hope.

"No more bein' beholden to the whims of others," said Mort. "Right, pal?"

Tap, tap. Tap, tap.

At least a minute crawled by while Jack stared off into the distance, the darkness, almost like he could see something Mort couldn't, until finally he said, "When it's all said and done."

The moon hung overhead, bright enough to lead the way, but leaving just enough shadows to keep Mort and Jack hidden as they snuck through the deserted streets.

Soundlessly, they slipped into Meyer's Cooperage. The scent of blood still hung in the air, tinged with something more earthy and unpleasant. A smell which hadn't been there the night before.

Mort shook it off, studying the room for anything out of place. Nothing appeared moved.

"We look everywhere," he whispered. "'Til the sun starts peekin' in. It's down to luck they ain't noticed him missing yet. Highly doubt we'll get another day of grace."

Jack nodded.

"Hey," he said, as something on the floor caught his eye. "It's that toothpick. Mort, it looks … charred, almost."

Mort stared a moment, then shook his head and set about his search.

Jack shrugged and kicked it away.

The building consisted of two rooms, one for stock and one for work. Meyer kept them clean and moderately organized. At Farrell's insistence, the two men moved every coffin, barrel, and wagon wheel in various states of completion, searching for an unsavory seam in the wood that might lead to a hidden stockpile.

The moon traveled across the sky, and they turned up not so much as a speck of untoward dust.

"Wild fuckin' goose chase, Jack. There ain't nothin' here."

Jack didn't answer. In one hand, he balanced a strange-looking tool, a half circle of wood with a metal edge and a peg jammed through the middle.

"What you got there?" Mort lifted his eyebrows.

"Don't know what it's called, but my daddy had one. I seen it used before," said Jack, with a faint smile. "Angle lines up with the rounded end of a barrel and you use it to cut a spot for the lid to fit. Nice and snug."

"All well and good," said Mort, burying the frustration in his voice. "What good's it do us, though?"

Without a word, Jack set across the room. A shiver raced up Mort's spine as he watched Jack mosey toward the watchful eye carved into the wood.

"Perfect circle." Jack pushed at the pupil of the symbol's eye with the tool's peg.

Pop.

A light clatter sounded from the other side of the wall. Mort stepped closer, eyes squinted. "Well? Don't just stand there. Give it another push?"

"Not a push. A spin."

With the peg anchoring the tool to the wall, Jack moved it around in a perfect circle, accompanied by a soft scraping noise as the tool traced the outline of the staring eye. Then the wood pulled free, just the right shape and size to top a barrel.

Jack lowered it to the floor with something like reverence while Mort struck a match. Both men leaned forward.

"Hold up a second."

Mort nearly jumped out of his skin at the big man's warning.

"Remember that odd black stuff? Sure seems like it wreaked unholy hell on that toothpick. We don't know what's in there. Could be gold, could be somethin' ugly. Somethin' we don't want to breathe in." Jack fished around in his pockets and removed two dusty bandanas. Tie this around your face and don't reach inside 'til we get a good look."

"Volatile," said Mort as he pulled the bandana tight and breathed in the musty smell. "That's the word Farrell used."

Jack furrowed his brows and pulled his own bandana snug. "Ready?"

Mort nodded, nothing to say for maybe the first time in his life. He let the match pass through the opening in the wall and watched its light flow over the contents of the chamber.

"Holy shit," he whispered, eyes going wide as the symbol on the wall. Wads of that same black gunk they'd found the day before stretched out along the length of the wall and down through the floorboards.

He looked up at Jack. Worry creased the skin around his friend's eyes. "What—"

"Gentlemen." A dandy voice floated across the room. "Kindly drop any weapons you might have and face us. Do it slowly."

The match fell from Mort's hand, disappearing into the cavernous darkness beyond the eye.

He turned to meet the piercing stare of Thaddeus Locke, the latest in a long line of sheriffs for Buzzard's Edge, and held his empty hands in the air. Next to him, Jack dropped the circular tool with a hollow *clunk* and raised his hands as well.

Behind the Sheriff, stood a tall, lanky man with shaggy hair. Mort couldn't think of his name but recognized him immediately as the fella who'd killed Noose Holcomb.

Vigilante rubbing elbows with the sheriff, thought Mort.

A young blonde girl, with a scar running down her cheek and a revolver in her hand, peeked out from behind the two men.

"My word," whispered Locke. His eyes shot like an arrow toward the young girl, then flew right back to Mort and Jack. "The girl was right. How did she know?"

The vigilante shook his head, but something in his eyes told Mort maybe he had an inkling. "If that's the case, then we best get them outta here, Thad, before …" He sniffed at the air. His gaze dropped to the floor and Mort followed it.

Smoke.

It seeped up between the floorboards in dark clouds. Before Mort could wrap his head around the phenomenon, plumes of flame raced like snakes along the seams between each plank of wood, rushing toward the walls and the wares.

"That ain't natural," whispered Jack.

"It's that black shit!" cried Mort.

Volatile.

"What is this?" cried Locke, unholstering his gun.

A wall of flame erupted from underneath the floor, separating Mort and Jack from their would-be captors. Wood splintered and embers roared.

"Floor's giving way!" shouted Mort.

From the other side of the fire, a gunshot boomed, splitting the cacophony. "Thad, No!"

The vigilante slapped the gun out of the sheriff's hand, and it clacked to the ground. Then everything grew quiet, like someone had placed their hands over Mort's ears.

Reflections of flame danced in the little girl's blue eyes as her face paled, and she backed toward the exit. Locke and the vigilante stood frozen in the doorway, unwilling to leave, horror etched across their faces.

"We've gotta go, Jack. Whatever's in the walls, the floor, it's some bad shit. Like gunpowder on mescaline." Mort stared into Jack's eyes over the bandana. They held a quiet calm, almost serenity.

"I don't think so." Jack let out a sigh, but there was no frustration in it this time. Only resignation. Like he'd just had enough of this life. He held up a trembling hand, covered in blood. In the flickering firelight, it appeared as black as the mess in Meyer's walls, the same shit currently sending the cooperage up in flames.

With a grunt, Jack sunk to the floor.

"Pressure," whimpered Mort. "We get some pressure on it and…" His eyes raced around the shrinking room, fire closing in on all sides. Hotter than the most scorching summer afternoon. "And we … We—"

"No," said Jack. "It's in my gut. I feel it. You stickin' around'd just drag us both beneath a heap of shit." He grimaced and blew out a series of quick breaths. "Go. Take care of yourself. I think I might like to … watch everythin' the two most powerful men in Buzzard's Edge want … burn."

The blaze surged all around them, louder than a blast of wind. Locke and his company no longer visible through the hellfire.

Mort grabbed Jack's arm and yanked, but it was like trying to tear a tree up at the roots. "That's fool talk. We can get you out. Said we'd land somewhere else, yeah? When all was said and done?"

"I said no, Mort." He shook his head. "Maybe Virginia Harvey did raise a couple of fools. But. This fool won't be tied to the whims of bad men no more. Tryin' to get ahead in this fucked up world." Jack leaned forward. "Besides … you really believe anyone gets out of Buzzard's Edge?" He held Mort's eyes for a moment, as if trying to pass an understanding Mort was too thick to receive. "Now, you better go. Otherwise, you ain't gonna have much of a choice. But to join me."

"Damn you," Mort spat through tears.

"I expect so," he said, with a smile that reached up and touched his eyes.

Mort ran for the window and tossed himself out through a burning curtain. A sickening crack from his shoulder cut through the bellowing fire, then he was up, fighting through the pain, and running for the saloon. A look over his shoulder saw the citizens of Buzzard's Edge pouring out of their homes to form a bucket brigade. Sheriff Locke and the vigilante stood at the head, a little more distance between them now. The young girl lingered behind them. For a second, she caught Mort's glance, a knowing look in her icy blue eyes.

When he reached the Saloon at the End of the World, Mort slammed the door shut behind him and collapsed on the floor. Though the atmosphere still contained the charge of a jubilant night, it was deadly quiet inside. All except for his labored breathing.

"Jack," he whispered, ripping the bandana off and tossing it aside. It had probably saved him some of the smoke inhalation, not to mention being recognized by the sheriff.

Tears cascaded down Mort's face and his breath came in hitching sobs. First, they came for the loss of Jack, his friend—hell, his only friend—then at the realization that Jack had surely thought of moments before he gave himself over to the fire.

Farrell would be furious.

And there would be no stopping what came next.

THE REAPING, PART IX

Sand skitters in, drinking the blood of Josiah Dennis with a low, almost sensual, groan.

Coyote scratches at its ear, trailing a line of rust red along its silver-gray coat. The feral look has left its eyes, giving way to a knowing intelligence. "Think that last story counts? It'll make its way into the earth as intended?"

"A fitting eulogy, if nothing else." Vulture swoops up to the top of the steps. Crimson stains still lining its beak, it carves letters one-by-one into the schoolhouse wall.

Josiah Dennis Schoolhouse, reads the impossibly tidy scrawl.

Vulture stares in silence as the last traces of Josiah's lifeblood vanish into the bone-white sand. It scrapes and scratches as it crawls over Josiah's body, covering the man like flies on a pile of shit. For a moment, the outline of his corpse remains, then it begins to sink, almost fluttering down like a blanket in the wind. When the earth flattens, the dry burble of the sand fades away.

Like he was never there, thinks Coyote.

"Now he is committed to the earth," intones Vulture. "And the stories with him. One to remain buried, perhaps lost forever. The others to germinate and attempt to grow in this arid hellscape."

"How long do we wait?" asks Coyote.

When Vulture speaks, there is a note of uncertainty in its voice. One that makes a chill race down Coyote's spine all the way to the tip of its tail. "I do not know."

Coyote narrows its eyes. "It's not comin' through clear?"

"I fear it's not coming through at all. All I see is you and a deserted town. As to what comes next, we can only hope we've done enough."

"That little girl in the last story," says Coyote. "It was Alice, wasn't it? What did Locke mean when he said she was right?"

Vulture's bald head wrinkled with concern. "Perhaps nothing, but I wonder the same. It could be that the sight is not lost but granted to another." A twinkle appears in Vulture's good eye. "Not for us to know, I suppose. It's possible we are not destined to live forever, that you and I will be naught but bone and rot by the time she is born."

Coyote remains silent, staring out toward the horizon. "Do you see that?"

With a flurry of wings, Vulture propels itself onto the schoolhouse's bell tower, narrowing its eyes west.

"Whatever it is, it's kicking up too much dust to make out clearly."

Coyote's lips pull up in the guise of a grin. "It worked."

Vulture flutters back to the ground, lets out a caw-like laugh. "It certainly appears that way. There is misery ahead, my friend, but by the stars, there will also be life."

AFTERWORD

What you hold in your hands is more than three years of my imagination populating this small Arizona town with loathsome creatures and hope. The idea was always to expand the possibilities of what could be done with the western genre, if I wasn't compelled to stay within the genre. Hence why you just read tales of vampires, creature features, whodunnits, and talking animals all within the same backdrop.

I can only say I sincerely hope you've enjoyed your time in Buzzard's Edge. If this is your first trip, there's more to see, some of it already available in bookstores everywhere, and there's also more to come. If you're a fan of story notes, I've included some brief thoughts below, and if you jumped to story notes before stories, beware, they do contain spoilers.

They Only Come Out at Night: This story started out with the idea of a gang of vampires in mind, truly mixing that outlaw, wild west quality with supernatural creatures. Quickly, it transformed around the hinge of, what if that whole myth about a vampire needing an invitation to enter your home extended to a town line? How would they go about getting that invitation, and what would happen once it was spoken aloud? Violet Conway and Ned Callaghan were fun characters to write, and I very much enjoyed their dynamic.

Come and Take My Hand: I've written a fair bit of short fiction, and this one has a special place in my heart. Maybe it's even my favorite. Who's to say? I almost didn't write it, thinking maybe it humanized George "Noose" Holcomb a little too much. But I'm glad I did, because it has magic, wonder, darkness, and hope flowing through its veins, and those are all my favorite things to read. It was originally published in the trade paperback edition of *Noose*, as well as being offered through DarkLit Press's library of free ebooks. I included it here, because the overall story, wraparound included, just didn't feel complete without it. The title comes from a Thrice song called "Scavengers."

Holes: This was the first Buzzard's Edge story I wrote after *Noose*, originally intended for a splatterpunk western anthology that never came to fruition. The idea originated as part of a 31 days of Halloween Twitter event to fit a horror story into 240 characters or less.

"What started as a nuisance, a few small holes in the backyard, is really starting to worry me. They just keep growing, black voids descending to God knows where. I haven't seen the dog since yesterday and the scratching from under the floorboards won't stop."

Josh Malerman commented to say it was a cool idea, and I went on to combine it with the idea of a lawman suffering from PTSD in an unholy mix of Stephen King's "The Raft" and Poe's "The Tell-Tale Heart". This story first appeared in the anthology *Hot Iron and Cold Blood*, edited by Patrick R. McDonough.

Where the Daybreak Ends: Readers who spent time with *The Demon of Devil's Cavern* will likely recognize this story. Oddly enough, I wrote this more than a year before I started that book, and just happened to stumble upon the perfect place to reference Andrew and Wes. Of course, people who've read my work outside of Buzzard's Edge will find some not so tongue-in-cheek references to the *Slattery Falls* trilogy in Robert Weeks and the phantoms. Truth be told, linking these stories was a lot of fun. I also loved the title of this one—borrowed from the song (appropriately) "A Hole in the World" by Thursday—enough to make it the title of the collection.

Trade Secrets: I am a massive Sherlock Holmes fan, and when I started dreaming up stories (at the time) unrelated to Rory Daggett, but set in the old west, I knew I needed my own consulting detective. I did not know until I neared the end of this story that he was also a serial killer. Thaddeus Locke has become a favorite character to write, and perhaps most interesting to me is the way "Trade Secrets" and *The Demon of Devil's Cavern* can be read and enjoyed separately, although each adds more layers to the other. If you previously read *DoDC*, this tale makes Locke's actions much more interesting. This story originally appeared in *Blood in the Soil, Terror on the Wind*, edited by Kenneth W. Cain.

Salvia Sunset: This story was originally written for *The Horror Collection: Monster Edition*, edited by Kevin J. Kennedy. By the time I received that invitation I'd written a fair few Buzzard's Edge stories, but hadn't tried my hand at a creature feature yet. Nola Betts takes her namesake from author/editor/reviewer, Candace Nola, who also edited this book, and likely wouldn't hesitate to take down a monster that a big, loud group of men unleashed and couldn't control. The initial idea for this story revolved around werelizards, and although it never really materialized, I just may have to write that someday. The last three paragraphs are original to this printing of the story.

The Ice Man: Surely, I couldn't write all these stories set in Buzzard's Edge and not include Rory and Alice. I always knew they'd get a story in here. I just didn't know it'd be novella length and stray from the supernatural into something more like a Law and Order-type procedural, with that revenge aspect from *Noose*. I love how this story allowed me to explore the time between *Noose* and *DoDC*, digging into the origin of Rory and Alice's sign language and their relationship with Billy Chambers. If *DoDC* didn't cement Alice as my favorite character to write in all my fiction, "The Ice Man" definitely did the trick. I hope you enjoyed reading it as much as I enjoyed writing it.

When It's All Said and Done: This is a bit of an odd one, and although I think it stands on its own two legs, it's the closest thing to pure connective tissue this collection has, referencing events in the other books, but generally leaving them as a backdrop. Through the eyes of two Lansdalian criminals who, deep down, want to be decent, we see what Buzzard's Edge looks like after the events of *The Demon of Devil's Cavern*, and leading up to the upcoming third book laying out Rory and Alice's story. Though I haven't written that book as of yet, I've got the first chapter outlined and some notes on what happens next. Folks, it's going to be a doozy. If you're intrigued and you've already read this far, don't skip the last page of this book.

The Reaping: Ever since the first visit to Buzzard's Edge, when the line about the sand drinking blood poured out, I always found the idea about the land being as alive and wicked as the people in it fascinating. When I pitched this collection, I knew one of the stories would be something of an origin for the town. Although this story didn't quite go back to the very beginning of history, I kind of like this better. I had a lot of fun playing with time and space, confusing poor Josiah before I eventually had him meet his maker. I've also always wanted to write something with anthropomorphic animals, so there's another box checked. I borrowed the title from a Coheed & Cambria song, and I swear you can almost hear that opening acoustic guitar riff when Josiah Dennis steps into the sun for the first time.

The end of a book wouldn't be complete without a few thank you's. Some of the people who made this possible were Heather and Steve at Brigids Gate, Val Halvorson for a third (and hopefully not final) remarkable cover, Tyler Jones for a generous and undeserved introduction, Candace Nola for regular reminders to breathe, as well as insightful edits, Erica Robyn and Patrick R. McDonough for always being there. A tremendous thank you, as well, to anyone who has read one of these books, taken the time to shout about it, and to any reader who found something to connect with, especially in Alice. She means the world to me too.

About the Author

Brennan LaFaro is a music teacher by day, horror writer by night, living in southeastern Massachusetts with his wife, two sons, and his hounds. He is the author of the *Slattery Falls* trilogy, the *Buzzard's Edge Saga*, as well as *Illusions of Isolation* and *Last Stay*. You can read his short fiction in various anthologies and find him on Twitter at @brennanlafaro or at www.brennanlafaro.com.

LAGNIAPPE

During a staff meeting one gloriously stormy night, the idea of having a "Lagniappe" near the end of some of the works published by Brigids Gate Press was discussed. The staff unanimously voted in favor of the idea.

Lagniappe (pronounced LAN-yap) is an old New Orleans tradition where merchants give a little something extra along with every purchase. It's a way of expressing thanks and appreciation to customers.

The Lagniappe section might contain a short story, a small handful of poems, or a non-fiction piece.

***

For the lagniappe for this book, the author decided to throw in an extra story, *Spokes in a Wheel*, for all of his readers. Hope y'all enjoy it!

Spokes in a Wheel

Moses Harvey leaned out over the balcony of his rooms at the Scarlet Revolver. A few streets over, smoke, as black as the abyss, drifted into the sky, marring the first rays of sunlight.

Across the room, his door creaked open, and Alexander Farrell stepped inside, carrying two glasses of amber liquid, a chunk of ice floating in each one.

"You should sit," he said.

Harvey turned with a glare, then returned his gaze to the streets below. "That sure looks like it's coming from Meyer's place," he said.

Farrell handed Harvey one of the glasses, then sipped his own. The mayor downed half his glass in a single gulp.

"It's a total loss, then," said Harvey.

"Yet to be seen," said Farrell. "I'll get to the point, Moses. By the time they put it out, there was still a body inside. Judging by the … size, seems like it was Jack. I'm sorry, my friend."

Moses inhaled deeply, then squeezed the glass until it popped, raining down shards of ice, glass, and blood on the street below.

"The little fella is still alive?"

"Mort. If he hasn't skipped town." Farrell cleared his throat. "You should know Jack was gutshot before he, uh, burned up."

Harvey nodded. "Bring Mort here before he takes a mind to run off. Those two seemed thick as thieves. I don't expect that little shit killed my brother, but I bet he knows who did." He huffed, then mumbled, "Shit doesn't go that wrong, that fast, without a little help. There's others who put a spoke in Jackie's wheels, and when I find out who … we'll make 'em hurt."

Farrell smirked and backed out of the room, leaving Mayor Harvey staring out over Buzzard's Edge once more, half his face bathed in shadow.

MORE FROM BRIGIDS GATE PRESS

Melinda West: Monster Gunslinger

KC Grifant

KC Grifant comes out guns blazing with *Melinda West: Monster Gunslinger*—a devious action-packed adventure set in a very weird version of the Old West. Fast, furious, and a hell of a lot of fun!"—Jonathan Maberry, NY Times bestselling author of *Son of the Poison Rose* and *Relentless*

In an Old West overrun by monsters, a stoic gunslinger must embark on a dangerous quest to save her friends and stop a supernatural war.

Sharpshooter Melinda West, 29, has encountered more than her share of supernatural creatures after a monster infection killed her mother. Now, Melinda and her charismatic partner, Lance, offer their exterminating services to desperate towns, fighting everything from giant flying scorpions to psychic bugs. But when they accidentally release a demon, they must track a dangerous outlaw across treacherous lands and battle a menagerie of creatures—all before an army of soul-devouring monsters descend on Earth.

Supernatural meets *Bonnie and Clyde* in a re-imagined Old West full of diverse characters, desolate landscapes, and fast-paced adventure.

BLOOD ON THE SOIL, TERROR ON THE WIND

Ed. Kenneth W. Cain

Whether in an old weathered mine shaft, somewhere off the beaten path, out in the woods, or right here in the middle of this ghost town, danger awaits. We're going to take you way back, drop you right smack dab in the middle of the Old West at its finest. But we're not just going to give you shootouts and bullet wounds and blood splatter. Yes, those things are prominently featured, but there's so much more to this anthology of western horror.

Maybe it's a well-known creature popping in for a visit, or some new creepy crawly monster sucking out your soul, we're going to turn the Old West inside-out and explore its guts to the fullest. There are new adventures to be had, monsters both familiar and unfamiliar to be thwarted… And we're not always going to be the victors. Life in the Old West is hard, trying at its best, and it can wear you down quick.

So, prepare yourself to be transported back in time. Get yourself up on that rickety stagecoach, draw your guns, and let's get going. There's vast territory to cover here, and your journey begins now.

THE PRISONERS OF STEWARTVILLE

Shannon Felton

Stewartville. A town living in the shadow of the prisons that drive its economy. Haunted by the ghosts of its past. Cursed by the dark secrets hidden beneath. A town so entwined with the prisons waiting outside the city limits that it's impossible to imagine one without the other, or to ever imagine escaping either.

When a teenage boy digs into the history of the town, he discovers a tunnel system beneath Stewartville, passageways filled with dark secrets. Secrets leading not to freedom, but to unrelenting terror.

Stewartville. Where the convicts aren't the only prisoners.

SHADOW OF THE HIDDEN

Kev Harrison

It's Seb's last day working in Turkey, but his friend Oz has been cursed. Superstition turns to terror as the effects of the ancient malediction spill over and the lives of Oz and his family hang in the balance. Can Seb find the answers to remove the hex before it's too late?

From Kev Harrison, author of *The Balance* and *Below*, journey with Seb, Oz and Deniz across ancient North African cities as they seek to banish the

Shadow of the Hidden.

Visit our website at: www.brigidsgatepress.com